FREE RIDER
(A SYMBIOSIS)

JANET PORTER

Free Rider by Janet Porter

Cover illustration by Priscilla Kim
Cover design by Julie Metz Design
Interior design by Amy Sumerton

All inquiries should be addressed to:
TKO Studios, LLC
1325 Franklin Avenue
Suite 545
Garden City, NY 11530

TKO STUDIOS is a registered trademark

Visit our website at tkopresents.com

First Edition
ISBN: 978-1-952203-90-9

Printed in the United States of America

This book is for every poet and writer—dead or otherwise—who has whispered to me over these many years, embedding themselves in my subconscious. The result of those whisperings is now released into the wind.

It is for my late father, reluctant warrior-class hero, delver, poet, and stranger in a strange land, whose self imposed mission was to get to the bottom of it all, to extract art from pointless suffering. It is for all those who expressed the agony, the ecstasy, and the day-to-day danse macabre through music and lyrics. The palette you have all provided— its hue and tone—is virtually limitless when you begin to tap into and immerse yourself in it.

Mostly, I hope you enjoy this effort, on whatever level. But for all who might be offended, please don't sue me; I'm broke.

FREE RIDER
(A SYMBIOSIS)

They remain dead, the people I try to resuscitate by straining to hear what they say. But the illusion is not pointless, or not quite, even if the reader knows all this better than I do. One thing a book tries to do, beneath the disguise of words and causes and clothes and grief, is show the skeleton and the skeleton dust to come. The author too, like those of whom he speaks, is dead.

—Jean Genet

Flectere si nequeo superos, Acheronta movebo.
(If I cannot bend those above to my will, make Acheron do my bidding.)

—Virgil's *Aeneid*, book VII.312

PROLOGUE

Lieutenant Mark Vincente
July 23, 1985

I need to walk it back to the beginning—if that was the beginning. If not, where was it? Whatever the motive was behind the Westchester carnage is getting more and more obscure, like everything that happened before and after it. Do I even want to know anymore? Does Bruno? Anyway, isn't that the joke about the bad guys—that they only kill each other? Bruno and I don't joke about this one, though. There's something else hovering around the blunt force details of murder. We're both chin deep in this now, and the hard line between right and wrong is getting blurrier every day. We're dancing around an idea that I never would have thought possible a handful of months ago. Neither of us wants to lay it out on the table though—not yet.

I think of all the random mayhem I can't keep up with—that nobody can—how it echoes into the future   inspires others to follow in the bloody footprints.

Where do those footprints lead if you follow them for the next ten, twenty years?

Ask not for whom the sirens scream . . .

I think, now, that Violet never had a chance. Maybe I didn't either.

I think maybe it's deeper and dirtier than I—or any of the clean up squad—can ever get to the bottom of . . . or would want to.

I specialize in the cesspit that is vice. I dive in with a single mission: identify and collect the wormiest heads, slowly and methodically, with the persistence and intent of a hell hound. I imagine placing those skulls in a display case with all the meticulous attention the slicer, the gouger, the burner might lavish on his victims: "This one is from 1989; this, from 1991," and so on, until I give out completely, or become one of them in my own head—its back roads crawling with the same worms, maggots—contaminated by them—beyond the reach of reason. I would gaze into the bottomless void behind the gaping holes where their eyes, black and remote as deep space, once fastened upon their victims. I would contemplate their dirt-filled mouths, twisted in a final shriek of agony, or surprise at how quickly Death ran them down, displayed to the defilers its hideous steely mask, more implacable, more pitiless than their own. They would stare into his dead-oyster eyes, smell his decay as he enfolded them into his gaping jaws, shook and flung them onto the mound of bone and carrion, as ancient as the history of the human race itself.

I would do all this with the discernment of a buyer of masterworks in some uptown art gallery, except I would be the master. Art, somebody said, should strive to tell the truth the way the artist sees it. I would splash the canvas, mold the clay with that truth—the righteous terror, the suffering that saturated the final moments of my unspeakable subjects. I would line my walls with these, review them over and over as my discerning eyes scan the gallery walls, the pedestals displaying the demented, twisted sculpture. I would speak to them as if they could hear me.

But I am a cop, and I got into this exclusive club by suppressing every inkling of these aberrant visions. Didn't I? I admit this now, to myself, because it's the truth. I am a man first, a cop second. I do the work as if only the truth matters. And it does, if it leads to real retribution. I will always believe this, with or without the badge. I have lost all that made the world tolerable, as it spins ever closer to the twenty-first century after Christ. I have lost what might have allowed even a sliver of light to seep into the horror dungeon, the torture chamber in my head. There is nothing for me in a new millennium but more of the same.

I remember the ending of an Auden poem Violet recited from memory, not long after our first meeting, how mundane evil, the grotesque, happens—right along with the sacred, the songs of birds, the prayers flung at Shakespeare's deaf heaven. I even remembered reading it once in school, how it affected me, what it means now:

> *In Breughel's Icarus, for instance: how everything turns away*
> *Quite leisurely from the disaster; the ploughman may*
> *Have heard the splash, the forsaken cry,*
> *But for him it was not an important failure; the sun shone*
> *As it had to on the white legs disappearing into the green*
> *Water, and the expensive delicate ship that must have seen*
> *Something amazing, a boy falling out of the sky,*
> *Had somewhere to get to and sailed calmly on.*

Will technology even the playing field or make it more virulent?

Before everything that conferred meaning was carved out, there were moments of solace that would sneak up unawares—early in the morning or at dusk—border moments—oases in time where iron-fisted reality took a break. In these moments, I once found the will to plow on, dive again into the yawning, stinking black abyss. I know Violet had those moments as well—but too few to make a difference.

My family: I know now that I would gladly barter whatever remains of my humanity if I were permitted the faintest glimpse, could hear the smallest echo of what is slowly receding; memory overtaken and consumed by cold necessity, by the insistent pulse and heat of life, by what's around the next corner. I don't know with what forces I might align myself if given the opportunity to fulfill a shadow mission, how I might stain my soul beyond recognition or redemption.

I would do it, I think sometimes, without regret. Maybe with pride. Pride in my art.

I didn't start out questioning Violet. A homicide detective, Lorena Bruno, did. But when loose ends needed tidying, when pieces wouldn't fit, I paid Violet a visit down in funky Soho. She had no phone, so I just showed up there in the trickster hours where I once found respite. Funny how you never know where or when that door will open—the one you enter and fall into yet another alien universe, one from which you'll never really emerge.

There may have been some who have mistaken my placid exterior for equivocation. This usually worked in my favor.

Nothing works anymore. And yet, here I am going over my notes again, the bare facts that never reveal what bubbles underneath.

Yeats got it right: "Things fall apart; the center cannot hold . . . the blood dimmed tide . . . the ceremony of innocence. Drowned."

I have lost Violet and I can't find Khalika. But maybe that phantom has found me. And if she wants my soul, I'm not sure I don't want to give it to her.

ACT I

I turned silences and nights into words. What was unutterable, I wrote down. I made the whirling world stand still.
—Arthur Rimbaud

CHAPTER 1

Of two sisters, one is always the watcher, one the dancer.

—Louise Glück

August 1984

Right before Sylvia Plath stuck her head in the oven, she wrote one of her best poems. Then she paid for it. She sounded pretty satisfied that a stake had been hammered into her daddy's fat, black heart. I mean, even the *villagers* never liked him. She was through with the bastard.

I'm through too. And it didn't take that long. You've gotta admit that when Sylvia found her voice, she didn't mess around. I'm getting there, I think. At least Khalika said so.

Can a name contain a destiny? After all, I was always the "shrinking violet." Khalika is all that I am not. But I take comfort in the idea that things are evening up now. She needs me too. I'm her foil, her straight girl. I'm the project she can't let go—the one that will never be quite wound up. She's the poem that keeps haunting me, its meaning both occulted, yet stunningly clear—like a Zen riddle. It whispers to you in that land between sleep and wakefulness.

"Just give it to me from the beginning, Violet," said Detective Lorena Bruno, referred to hereafter as DB. "Anything you remember, even small stuff."

I was willing to accommodate . . . to a point. It didn't look like DB was gearing up for a deep dive, but one never knows. She already had her little damaged orphan fish, gasping on the sand; it was pretty clear she had no intention of filleting it and eating it raw.

In my life *pre*-blood bath, I would have been a basket case. But it was a different universe now. Twenty was sneaking up on me, and I could talk to anybody, including—if I could

11

get an appointment—whatever psycho gods were running this place. I could let them know what fuck-ups I thought they were for letting all these crazy monkeys—apes, to be precise—make such a wholesale shit heap of the planet. I guess it's that "free will" thing—you know—the one nobody seems able to agree even exists?

Anyway, I've decided to pretend it does. I mean, what else can you do in a world where you might not even be in control of what you're going to think about next?

I could almost see DB writing "the inside story" in her head—the one she'd have time to write after she retired and needed an income boost. No, this one wasn't setting me up to break me down. She would tread lightly, transfer me, and set me up in a nice, warm tank with rocks and ferns.

Who could tell this story anyway? Maybe only Khalika.

Sherlock Holmes, in the famous "Holmesian fallacy," said that after eliminating what can't be true, then whatever remains, however improbable, must be it. That might work in detective stories; in reality, you need omniscience—a god—or a deus ex machina intervention. Occam's razor has to go too—not multiplying things beyond necessity to shore up a theory. The simplest explanation, the least layered one, sometimes just doesn't cut it.

And that's pretty much the story of our lives, maybe anybody's.

Ordinary folk secretly love hearing about the tragedies of others—as long as the splatter never hits them. This story gets way beyond the splatter though, into territory usually closed off to the readers, the watchers, the voyeurs who sit in their recliners, deck chairs, the darkened theatres—waiting for that vicarious thrill. As long as it keeps its distance, doesn't claw itself up a tree in a neighbor's backyard and stare intently into the bedroom window. This story, if it could be told, would send them scurrying under their beds, children who realize they won't be waking from this nightmare. This cop won't get to write it either; even I struggle with how this all came to be, how to untangle the skein. I have no clue when it started, and I don't think Khalika does either.

Bad guys are, for the most part, fucking stupid, which is why you see them giving the finger to the security camera that eventually identifies them, and also why you can get so much information in bars like Naked Envy. The ones who did the hit at the Westchester house were stupid . . . or wanted to look like they were. They left calling cards, Khalika said, signatures—but no prints. Then there's the other brand of batshit psychos, the ones Khalika—she's my twin, by the way—loves to study. They're the ones who do it for fun, who get better with practice. Some of these overachievers aren't exactly stupid; they're cunning, methodical, like arachnids. Like Dick and Bianca. They're shapeshifters who can blend into any crowd, where they might carefully watch how "regular Joes" run their games. And just when you think it can't get any darker, it does. Much darker. It's called snuff. It's the coinage of the brains behind pa and ma—Dick and Bianca. Did it exist even before film? I say it did. Khalika says it did.

"Just start like you're . . . telling a story. Some parts might be hard to remember, like a dream—kind of foggy. Others will be clearer."

She really wanted the back story, how I managed to emerge semi-functional from this, how it remained hidden for so long—like a malignant tumor—curled up and metastasizing—like all future serial killers—in the darkness of the womb.

She wanted to know when I knew what Dick and Bianca were up to. They'd met in high school, started with petty grifting, moved up to long cons. Further up the Hadean highway, they sanitized the tainted cash (*isn't it* all *tainted if you follow it back far enough?*), and—finally—the kiddie porn, kidnapping, and sex slavery. Snuff was just the logical destination, the terminus of that train. It took stamina, ruthlessness, and a shared vision—more than even the Wall Street boys have. These two were the ultimate soulless soulmates, willingly boarding the train together.

DB slipped on the grooming glove. The empathy was there, snuggled up to the need to get the dope. She knew trauma when she saw it: flat affect, monotone, no blubbering.

Little did she know that I just didn't give a shit, could hardly keep from bursting out laughing at her grave demeanor.

I'm all about the truth now—as *I* see it, even if nobody else does, even if this cop doesn't. Until the thing that knocked the planet even further off its wonky axis, I would never have thought the way I do now. But the thing had been taking root in the dark, blooming, before the pods burst open, scattered to the winds. I can hardly remember who I was before, when I was afraid to say shit if I had a mouthful.

So, sitting there on the bed in that swanky hotel, propped up by the fifteen pillows these places always seem to provide, I told DB we might as well get to the main event. She put a finger to her lips and leaned in with her notepad, her eyes soft with studied compassion. So I gave her some of what she thought she wanted.

"I'm just surprised it didn't happen sooner. I'd always assumed the door would be battered in by the cops instead of Dick's business associates, but they beat them to it. Of course, the door wasn't *battered in* at all. Somebody let them in. The killers waited for the signal. I heard Dick on the phone a few times talking about new recruits—the younger the better, the less family the better."

It's those families that cause all the trouble; they keep looking for the disappeared ones. "We just want closure," they say to the camera as their eyes brim with tears. They say this because they see others saying it on TV. They don't know what else to say. "We just want to bring her home."

I paused, gauging her reaction: alert, concerned, a little bird-like. I forged ahead.

"I've actually known what Dick was up to since I was ten or eleven, but I just ignored it. He left his porn right out in the open, like he was proud of the hobby he turned into a burgeoning business."

Cut to the chase rustled through my head like a strong breeze wafting the odor of a feedlot in the heart of Texas.

"When it all went down, I was in the barn, didn't hear any commotion. Next thing I knew, cops were waking me up in the morning, beer cans surrounding me, Mercutio—my horse—all agitated, his cat trying to calm him down." DB regarded me quizzically. "Really, Mercutio has a cat! And now, here we are. These guys were real ninjas, huh?"

I could tell DB thought this strange—that I'd heard nothing that night, that even Mercutio wasn't alerted. After all, they found Dick with his own dick in his own ugly potato trap, his severed pinky finger stuck up Bianca's glory hole, imperial jadeite-and-diamond ring still on it. Nothing was ransacked either. These folks weren't into robbery—mayhem only.

I took a sip of my tea and a bite of toast, went quiet for a few moments. DB waited, pen poised. I thought about what Khalika said: that the dumbasses made so many mistakes, it was comical—severing parts premortem, ensuring fonts of blood.

"Maybe they slid down in it too, took pratfalls. You know, like in some really black comedy?"

She laughed then, kind of involuntarily.

"Maybe they filmed it. You know, why should anything go to waste."

I told DB it looked like the ones who organized it wanted as much fear and pain inflicted as possible, that they didn't care how gory it got. Maybe they wore plastic garbage bags. Those guys—the ones who ordered the double hit—cruise around in such deep, dirty water they can't get off to run-of-the-mill gore porn anymore, if they ever did. But they sure know what motivates their customers, what they'll pay a king's ransom for. They must have instructed their envoys to pose them, bent over the Lucite coffee table, like pornographic puppets.

DB was riveted, as much by the subtext as my deadpan delivery. She stared at me, mesmerized. I dabbed my lips with my napkin and asked if she minded if I dialed up room service for some beer and a pack of smokes. She was a little startled but agreed. I don't get stupid when I drink, by the way—only more focused.

Still, I wished Khalika would hurry and get back. I really needed her input, even if she thought I was fine handling things myself now. I love Khalika. I never would have made it this far without her. She'll show up exactly when she needs to.

"Maybe I'll order a sandwich too."

CHAPTER 2

After room service delivered, I popped a beer, took a few sips, and continued. No smokes, but I'm not really addicted anyway.

"What else can I say? I mean, you already know the housekeeper, Lupe, found them the next morning, tried to run back out, got woozy, passed out, and cracked her head on the counter on the way down—so they sent an ambulance for her too, along with the meat wagon. The barn is at least a hundred yards from the house. But you know all that too. I took some Heinekens from the fridge that night. Beer always puts me to sleep," I lied. "That and horse sounds. I sleep in the hayloft."

I went on, feigning weariness despite being a little wired.

"Earlier that night, Dick said—at the dinner table—to, and I quote, 'Get the fuck out of my sight,' and so I did what I was going to do anyhow. After dinner the two of them usually went off to separate areas of the house, or out again, doing whatever it was they did. When Bianca slept, it was with Prince Valium, or whatever else was in the cabinet. Or the happy housewife stomped off to meet one of her boy or girl toys—maybe both at once."

The truth is, I never wanted to know what they did. I only wanted to get away from their shit. Aside from what they were into, they were like two vampires bickering over who or what to suck the life out of next. What most people don't realize is how *dull* rich people are, especially the nouveau kind, the kind who'll do anything for enough loot to get them into the inner sanctums of the old-money blood drinkers. They really are—boring and evil at the same time. Because they're almost always mean and conniving, people get the idea that they're fascinating, that they'd just love to hear all about their insider sex and money dirt. Lots of regular people would love to be that vicious too—in so many more stimulating ways—if they only had the time and money. If they weren't too busy making ends meet and fucking up their kids. I can't remember when I figured that out. Maybe it was even before I met up with Dollar Man.

I know. "Who's that?" you're about to ask. I'm getting there. *Patience.*

DB looked up from her scribbling. You could almost hear her thinking that no teenager should talk like this, should know this much. But I knew of at least one other girl who did—who does: my sister, my twin. I stared at the blank TV screen and lifted my palm, as if to clear the dark glass, sweep aside that painted veil separating what passes for reality and the engine of orderly chaos that operates behind it. *Chaos and order . . . hot ice . . . wondrous strange snow. Khalika.*

I conjured that evening, then the moonless night, the event horizon before the morning that sucked it all down that voracious black hole, then puked me up in this new universe where I had to start from scratch again, to reinvent, restructure my narrative.

"It was after dinner, so both of them were pretty shitfaced off a couple of bottles from the wine cellar, and they started sniping at each other. It was SS/DD."

I figured she would get the abbreviation, and she did.

"Bianca didn't care where the money came from to stock that cellar, her closets, her jewelry vault—only that it flowed at the same rate as Victoria Falls. They have his and hers Manhattan condos. Sorry, I mean *had.*"

DB tipped so far forward on her chair that she almost lost her balance.

"Dick interviewed his modeling hopefuls in his. Bianca entertained a steady stream of bisexuals. Dick was all man though, at least in his habits. Whatever 'man' means."

I laughed then; I couldn't help it. I didn't mention that Khalika knew about Bianca's wide-ranging tastes by listening in on a few of her phone calls, and by tailing her. Him too.

"By the way," I added, nonchalantly, "did you know I always had a feeling they conspired and then murdered my real father, JeanLuc DeLoache, for his money? It's quite romantic, huh? My birth mother, Oceane, died a week after I was born. Sepsis."

DB's face registered shock before she collected herself, asked if I had any other family.

"Nope, I've always had those two lovebirds all to myself."

I guess it's obvious now that I never mention Khalika if I can help it, unless she's given me the OK. She prefers it that way—an element of surprise that might come in handy at some point. She'd left the Westchester house as soon as possible—laid low and lived off grid, for so long now. We were thirteen when she ran away in the fall of 1978 and even though we're technically legal adults now, I still avoid talking about her. Why should I? It only complicates matters.

I made a mental note to remember the boxes of papers that Khalika stored in the hay loft when I went back. She always told me we'd open them when the time was right, and she never steered me wrong.

They say smart cops don't ask questions they don't already know the answers to, but I don't think she saw any of this coming.

"If you check it out, JeanLuc's death was deemed a suicide, which actually kind of made sense, since he made the tragic mistake of marrying Bianca and living with the ice-cold, greedy bitch for three years. Of course, it's too late to reopen it now. She had him cremated before the body was cold."

I stared into the middle distance for a moment, for effect.

Finally: "It doesn't even matter anymore. I hardly remember him."

But that's another lie, Daddy. I think of you all the time—dream of you. I've imagined finding your consciousness somewhere in space time. I'd tell you how those two fuckers were defiled before being sliced open like rotten melons. Would your spirit find peace, or would you be horrified—repulsed by the violence and my joy at their obliteration? It's done though, was always going to be done, and it is beautiful in my eyes.

"Needless to say, I don't remember all that much of the earliest stuff—not consciously anyway. After all, I was a mere infant."

But I do have a vague memory of Bianca's wicked stepmother smile, her big tombstone caps flashing, as she pinched my baby flesh—hard, but not hard enough to bruise—when we were alone. Not long after she and my father married, she hired another nanny. She quit the pinching when I learned to talk, to babble with Khalika. Maybe JeanLuc caught on that we were beginning to be afraid of her—at least that's what Khalika thought. When I asked Khalika if she remembered the pinching, she wouldn't discuss it. Her face went dark, brooding.

I had to wonder if maybe Bianca did something even worse to her, but I figured she would have told me by now. Khalika was always the rebellious one. And she could never hide her contempt for them—almost inviting their abuse. But early on, they seemed to be intimidated by her, by her unblinking stare.

Once we started crawling, the bitch liked to keep us separated. She hated it when we'd put our heads together and communicate in our special baby language. What she didn't count on was that thing twins sometimes do—conspire almost telepathically. Sometimes, when Bianca was particularly cruel, I'd just start screaming, non-stop. After a while, I could feel Khalika's presence and calm myself until JeanLuc arrived, sometimes with Khalika in his arms. He would set her down beside me, and all was well for a while as we held hands and went to sleep.

Another hazy memory, like the recollection of a dream: I was maybe three or four. I must have found some matches, managed to strike one and light the drapes in their bedroom on fire. I sat there watching the butter-yellow silk sheers go up in flames before my father ran in, grabbed me, took me outside, then put out the flames with a fire extinguisher. He brought Khalika, who'd been screaming, to me. I vaguely remember her little face, all contorted and red. Maybe, in my infant mind, I was trying to find a way to rid my father, rid all of us, of the virulent hag. Can a baby hate? I don't know, but it seems that was always the emotion I felt whenever I saw, or even thought of, Bianca and, later, Dick, and it only pulsed hotter and stronger as time passed.

Those warring twins—love and hate—don't they sometimes become inseparable—conjoined—if things get bad enough? It's the same with Khalika, except its pulse is stronger, more insistent, more demanding of action. Mine simmered on a low flame, lodged in my throat, and made it hard to swallow anything much except liquids. It's a blessing, we decided, that the two of them never created a dichotomy in us—that there wasn't even a shred of warped and twisted love to get in the way of the loathing—to obscure the narrow and fragile border that separated them.

Longing, or some kind of love, I suppose, is what I feel when I think of JeanLuc or Oceane—the father I hardly knew and the mother I never did. I know that after a time, the hatred and longing intertwined in me, like the vines on the south side of JeanLuc's old studio, a beautiful, beckoning structure, seemingly made of light. Entirely glass enclosed under a canopy of green. It sat about twenty-five yards from the main house. After the massacre, JeanLuc's artwork was confiscated by the bank and auctioned off. We didn't get to keep any of it. He was gifted, and I'm sure he was the source of Khalika's talent. She is, as he was, adept at transferring her anger and grief onto canvas, to give it the color and depth that time bleeds out of it.

It was in the studio that Khalika found the long-buried photograph of JeanLuc and Oceane's garden wedding ceremony; she put it with the other stuff we kept up in the hayloft. The photograph radiated happiness and hope—JeanLuc in his suit from some earlier era; Oceane in a white slip of a gown, holding a small bouquet of pale-pink Moon River peonies and baby's breath from the garden.

I tried to focus on DB, but it was getting more difficult. She asked if I was OK.

"Yeah. Anyway, Bianca, with Dick's help, long conned our father into marrying her after she'd been our nanny for a couple of years. I know—that tired, old daddy-gets it-on-with-nanny cliché. I'm guessing my father was in a very vulnerable state after losing Oceane."

I really was mystified about how Bianca managed to pull *that* one off. JeanLuc must have wanted to believe her act, that even if she wasn't Oceane, she'd do right by us. Bianca certainly polished her acting skills to reel him in, probably watched real mothers in the park. As I said, it's what psychopaths do—study actual humans to learn how they behave. All that money was a mighty motivator for Lady MacB—and her slimy accomplice. It took a bit of doing by her and Dicky boy to pull off, but their ravenous eyes were fixed on the prize. Khalika always claimed she had her figured out early on, maybe even before she was aware of it herself.

Bianca, saccharine-sweet when required, was a raptor. She watched us like one too. She cooed and fussed over me when JeanLuc was around. She cooked for him—all his favorites, took gourmet courses. Khalika found an old certificate in Bianca's bureau drawer.

"She managed to snare our still-grieving father, pulled it off like the merciless pro that she is . . . um, was. After Oceane died and they—um, allegedly—disposed of my father, Bianca waited what she thought was a decent interval before she and Dick got hitched in a sleazy Las Vegas chapel. There's a photo of them, smiling like possums eating poop, the succubus flashing the five-carat, emerald-cut rock, probably my mother's, but at least JeanLuc set up a trust fund for us. Then Dick slithered right in, and the rest is, well, what it is."

DB pursed her lips and shook her head sympathetically, scribbled on.

"All neat and tidy, huh? Except Dad never would have killed himself, even if he was grieving. He never would have left me, his art, his horses. He likely regretted what he'd done, even before he was murdered. Bianca started the devaluation process—you know—the standard thing narcissists do after they love bomb you. By that time, it was too late."

I glanced at DB. She wasn't bothering to look up anymore unless I paused.

"I do remember her tone changing with him, that he could never do anything right. Soon, the cooking stopped too. It was all takeout, until a cook-housekeeper was hired."

I got up, belched loudly, shrugged apologetically, and went to the bathroom. I was getting tired of this trip down Memory Lane, tired of talking. I hadn't talked this much since the last time Khalika showed up. Even if I spoke to my dad in my head, or to my mother, I didn't like to talk about them to anybody but Khalika. When I came back into the room, DB was still writing. I popped another beer, drank half of it in one go, and continued. I think DB was surprised at my tolerance for the stuff.

"I was just about to turn five when they did it. I think they decided they needed to do it before JeanLuc got a chance to change his will or start divorce proceedings."

They have your stuff, Daddy, but I don't care about that. If you hadn't provided for us, we would have found a way. Because we contain the DNA of you and Oceane—because that, above all else, is what is precious and irreplaceable.

My voice dripped with a hatred I could hardly contain anymore.

"I stand to inherit a tidy sum when I turn twenty-one. Of course, the two grifters knew this. They never adopted me, not legally. My name is DeLoache. As JeanLuc's widow, Bianca got legal guardianship—through the infinite wisdom of the state—when it was determined there were no other relatives. Neither one would have made the cut in the adoption process—too much incriminating junk in the metaphorical trunk to be ferreted out. There was plenty of loot to take care of me, practically speaking. That's pretty much all the authorities care about."

Khalika showed me your painting, Daddy, behind a screen in your studio. The bride decked out in her tacky designer wedding dress. The bride is Bianca. Except in place of her conniving face, beneath a sheer white veil, is a skull—a smiling death's head. Bianca's big white teeth are tinged with blood that has dripped and splattered her gown. Did you know what was coming? Did you sense it? Did your need to join Oceane triumph over your love for us?

I watched DB trying to keep up. She should have taken shorthand in high school.

"Case closed. Even with that juicy trust fund looming ever closer. Even with all the wildly flapping red flags."

I paused, reached automatically for the empty cigarette pack.

"Glad I don't have to go through life saddled with the Danzinger name, though. Now, even my parents' house is gone—everything except what my father provided for me—all squandered by two douches who outsmarted themselves. That greed thing, it's like shooting up—you need ever-increasing quantities, until nothing is enough. It's the same with porn, with any vice, with all the things people use to keep their minds off death, to keep the shadow at bay. You can never fill an empty vessel with a hole in the bottom."

All this was having its effect. I could hear her intake of breath when I added that, considering both of them were already dead, they'd be denied their guided tour through the court system for all their crimes, including the ones long dead and buried. I always liked to imagine them eating canned ravioli at prison canteen tables, being jeered at by their fellow diners. Especially satisfying were daydreams of Dick being ass-raped by gang bangers, his head held down in a filthy crapper.

But it's only one execution per bag of blood and guts, and this kind of justice seemed fair enough. Take them out before they find Jesus, get a mail-order law degree, marry a fan, fuck her against a wall while the guards look the other way, and knock her up.

Violet and Khalika DeLoache. Us against the dirty old retrograde world. And soon, there'll be enough money to navigate it, maybe do a little good out there before the fade to black.

CHAPTER 3

Dick had plenty of other enemies, that's for sure—including his on-the-books employees—so DB's interviews with them saved me the trouble of droning on about what a vicious, stupid sociopath he was. She didn't get into details, but she did mention that none of them were shy about giving examples of the oily charm and off-hand cruelty Khalika and I were all too familiar with.

They told her everything they knew, but even they didn't know about his side business.

Imagine those movies where you're set up to *really* hate the bad guy, right from the get-go. My sister saw him operating once—and only once—at his office. It was one of the few instances he did something with her. He took her to a shrink, and he must have been pretty worried about doing it, but she'd pulled a knife on Bianca during one of their arguments. Khalika started acting out around twelve, and Dick's threats didn't mean shit to her. Her antics escalated to where he needed to get a handle on it before we were taken away, or Khalika started cutting herself—or worse, reporting him. Of course, for that to happen, they'd basically have to catch him on film going down on one of us or vice versa.

Anyway, he took her for an evaluation by an expert in teen exorcisms. Just kidding—she was just a shrink.

The evaluation was terminated mid-way because Khalika simply wouldn't interact with the woman. Ten minutes in, she spit on the shrink's carpet, then ground her cigarette butt into it. This was exactly what Dick would have scripted. He apologized and said that perhaps another form of intervention might be necessary, or that he might send her off to boarding school for an attitude adjustment. The shrink told him that adolescent eruptions of this magnitude were not uncommon. And that was the end of it. He had to pay for a new carpet.

Khalika told me how pissed he was that he had to pay for the carpet and the full hour, even though it was cut short. Afterward, with him in a foul mood, they went to Dick's office, where she caught a load of him in action. Of course, she was only too happy to fill me in when she was delivered home.

Actually, she didn't so much tell it as act it out, like a movie scene, using different voices for the different characters. She typed it up later with, as she said, a cigarette between her teeth. Khalika and I love film, and it's better to think of some things as a script anyway. I mean, it's the only way to process most of the shit that goes on. I paraphrased for DB, inserted myself in place of Khalika, but here's, more or less, what Khalika typed up and stuffed somewhere in one of those boxes:

An Asshole out of Hell
By Khalika DeLoache
One Sheet: A big red asshole, with a dick shoved in it.

INT. Dick Danzinger's penthouse office suite, Manhattan. Daytime, July 1982. Cue "Bad to the Bone," by George Thorogood.

Elevator doors open on a meticulously groomed man accompanied by a sullen, smirking pre-teen. The man side-eyes an attractive girl with exposed cleavage, her smug face an advertisement of the surgeon's art. He leans in close.

                    DICK DANZINGER
     (whispering)
        If you did not already exist, I would
        need to put in an order with Zeus.

He pulls an embossed card from his jacket and
hands it to her. He flashes a chicklet smile.

                    DANZINGER
        Call me.

The girl, though flustered, is pleased and
self-consciously runs her fingers through
streaked-blond hair. The man exits quickly,
leaving the girl staring after him, glossed
lips slightly parted.

Danzinger's jaw is set, tanned face expressionless as he whooshes past the outer receptionist, goth teen in tow, and clicks through
two wide glass doors with "Danzinger Agency" lettered in black. He takes long strides,
passing an outer office secretary who's on the
phone, studying her green-varnished nails. She
looks up, startled. He ignores her, but then
remembers what he requires of her.

                    DANZINGER
        COFFEE! COFFEE! COFFEE . . . and get
        me a fruit salad with some yogurt on
        it . . . no, a green smoothie . . .
        chop-chop! Oh, and get the kid whatev-
        er she wants.

The two proceed farther into the tempera-

ture-controlled lair, the teen following at a
distance.

                    DANZINGER
     Fuck it! Cancel that, it's almost
     lunch and I have a look-see . . . I
     think. Some bimbette from Shitstain,
     Idaho . . . Asswipe, Indiana, some "I"
     state. They all sound alike, I mean
     the girls and the states.

                 ANOTHER SECRETARY
     (looking up from an open magazine, startled,
     also flustered, smiling weakly)
     Oh, good morning, Mr. D. Do you want
     your calls from yesterday and this
     morning or just yesterday? Your ac-
     countant called about five times, fran-
     tic. The bank called and said you
     don't have enough in your account to
     cover the checks Jennifer wrote last
     week to pay the taxes and fees on the
     condos. And some really rude guy who
     said . . . never mind, I can't say
     what he said, but he's called before.

                    DANZINGER
     Just give the goddamned list to Lisa
     and tell whoever called from the bank
     that he can blow me, and if anything
     bounces again . . .

Danzinger draws an index finger across his neck.

>   DANZINGER (CON'T)
> But ring Bernie in two minutes and put
> him through to Lisa. Jesus, I can't
> even take a piss in peace around here!
> COFFEEEEEE!

Danzinger sweeps past her. When he is out of
sight, she waits exactly two minutes, speed-di-
als the accountant, puts him through, then
jumps up to get his coffee, nearly tripping over
some fashion magazines stacked by her desk.

>   SECRETARY
>   (hissing)
>   Motherfucking asshole, eat my Tampax!

>   PASSING MAIL BOY
>   (whispering)
>   I heard that.

CUT TO:
Danzinger arriving in his assistant's office,
which is outside his. She is older and harder
looking than the outer two, wears a wide gold
bangle, large hoop earrings and a black silk
midi-dress with shoulder pads.

>   DANZINGER
> You're about to get a call from the
> Bernster, Lis. Just find out what he
> wants now. And who the fuck am I sup-
> posed to be having lunch with, and
> what time?

                    LISA
(expressionless, voice monotone)
I already know what he wants, Dick,
but I'll ask again. Lunch is one
o'clock at Liguria.

                  DANZINGER
Yeah, right. Just tell Bernie there'll
be an infusion any day now and to quit
getting his shit in a downpour. And
goddammit, I meant for you to book
Jams. Never mind, book me there for
dinner.

                    LISA
'Kay. You're having lunch with the
cowgirl you flew in from Iowa, the Miss
Cornhole . . . whatever, the one you
saw at some local contest?

She checks Dick's schedule as he puts his foot
up on her desk and inspects one of his Ital-
ian-made loafers, pulls a tissue out of a box,
wipes the shoe, and drops it on her desk.

                    LISA
Her name's Shaundra Kelly. That really unpleasant guy called again too
— wouldn't leave a name — said you'd
know. He also called me a useless, lying cunt.

                  DANZINGER
(snorting)
Sweet! I guess this one'll order her

steak chicken-fuckin'-fried with tater
tots, thousand island on her salad, or
maybe "vinegar-ette."

Danzinger makes air quotes around the word.

This one could maybe have potential if
she loses about half a ton. If the guy
calls again, just tell him I'm working
on it and to quit making threats, or —

The phone rings. Lisa curls her lip before she
picks up the phone, tapping her nails on her
glass-topped desk before giving the finger to
Danzinger's back.

> LISA
> Hey Bernie, sup this time in numbers
> hell?

The receptionist and outer office secretary both
show up with coffees, look at each other help-
lessly. Danzinger takes a mug from one of them,
takes a sip, and spits it back in the mug.

> DANZINGER
> Jesus fucking Christ — this tastes
> like it drained out of Tut's asshole!

Danzinger puts the cup down on Lisa's desk and
demands a fresh one from a new pot. Then he
retreats to his soundproofed inner sanctum. He
yells to Lisa, before he shuts the door, to arrange for the kid to be taken home in his limo.

The teenager has ordered nothing from the downstairs trattoria.

> LISA
> Just bring him another one, I'll take
> that one. Give me his calls, all of
> them, except the prick with no name.
> Oh wait, he doesn't leave a number.
> Bring me an overdose of something too,
> or a gun. And get these fucking roses
> out of here — they're all wilted.

CUT TO:

EXT. Liguria. Camera pans quickly up to a win-
dow, through which we can see Danzinger and
Shaundra being shown to a table in back.
Shaundra is dressed in her Midwest best.

> DANZINGER
> You look like a Nordic goddess in that
> ensemble. How was your flight?

Danzinger's smile, wide and blinding against
his tan, doesn't reach his eyes.

> SHAUNDRA
> Great, Mr. Danzinger, smooth as silk.

> DANZINGER
> Please, call me Dick.

> SHAUNDRA
> (flustered)
> Oh, OK . . . Dick. This place is just
> amazing. It feels like I'm in a dream

and I'll wake up back home any second!

                    DANZINGER
    You're not in Kansas anymore?

CUT TO:
INT. An upscale hotel room. Danzinger and
Shaundra are going at it, loudly and grossly.

CUT TO:
Danzinger in the shower.

                    DANZINGER
    (singing off key to "American Girl" by Tom
    Petty)
        Raised on . . . bacon, lots of it
        . . . and cream of corn, vats of
        it . . .

CUT TO:
A faceless woman showering, blood running off
her breasts, her taut stomach, down her legs,
her feet, and into the shower drain.

CUT TO:
EXT. Danzinger estate. Father of the Year ar-
rives in the driveway. He alights from limo,
not waiting for the chauffer to open the door,
orders him to stand by.

                  UNIDENTIFIED GIRL
        (out of frame)
        Heeeere's Ozzie! He must have "got-
        ten off" early today. Whaddya wanna bet
        he's in a good-ish mood, and extra

hungry? What are the odds he hands
us a wad of laundered cash and sug-
gests we go to a movie and stay out
as long as we like?

Fade to black.
END scene.

The scene dissolved when DB asked what that was about, the woman showering, the blood. I had to think about that for a moment, then made a stab at it. I was never sure of that myself.

I turned my head to face DB.

"I dunno. Foreshadowing maybe, about Bianca's involvement in his business?"

I see pornography as death. It has to end in death, because it has to get worse and worse for the customers to get hard, especially the older fuckers. Even Dick and Bianca knew this.

"Or maybe it was Bianca after she found out one of her favorite lovers cheated on her."

DB stared at me. I couldn't begin to read her expression, and I didn't care what she thought anyway. It didn't matter to me why Khalika put that shot in, but she always has her reasons, and they always make sense.

"Just kidding," I said. "I doubt old Binny had the energy or planning skills for something like that. Besides, she might have broken a nail."

DB smiled weakly. Did she think I was giving her the runaround? Hard to say.

Women need to be complicit in all the filth, like Bianca, for it to be such a huge business. Women must cooperate, Khalika said. And women produce the stuff too. She talked about the buyers of the end product, how the ante must always be upped.

Between you and me, I almost believe Khalika had lived before, many times maybe, before she was born with me. It was like she knew everything from really early on. She read voraciously too—even more than I did—from way back, before Shakespeare, back to Lucretius and earlier. She would feed me everything she picked up on her virtual trips through the centuries.

"I took a break last year." Then, as if remembering another vague dream—some wacky plan from a lost childhood: "I was supposed to start college this fall."

What will I do now, Daddy? It doesn't matter, does it? Not now, anyway.

Last year, Khalika and I read our brains out, went to the movies, talked about everything, everything we read and saw. I rode Mercutio every day. Khalika had been out of the house for a while, so I was hardly ever there either, and when we were, we were mostly hanging out in the barn.

I took a few more sips of beer. Movies: I absorbed all the tricks—loved quick cuts, foreshadowing, flashbacks and forwards, voice overs, unreliable narrators—everything that keeps the audience on their toes and on the edges of their seats. If I ever write a screenplay—Khali and I have a plan to do one together, someday—I'll use all of them, maybe try to invent new ones, if that's even possible. I love it when writers show you the girl slipping a gun or knife in her bag and you forget all about it until she shoots or stabs her lover or his wife. Or at least I always forget; Khalika remembers. She'll say, "Here comes that gun," and laugh her husky laugh. I'm into when an actor talks directly to the audience, breaking the fourth wall. I like flashbacks that show how the bad guy never grieved his murdered wife at all—ate like a pig after the funeral, visited his mistress, screwed his brains out. I love it when time gets compressed, reality distorted. Khalika always knows what's going on but never spoils it for me. I've gotten better at it—at knowing—and now we both look at each other at the exact moment we know who dunnit, or who's winding up with a toe tag.

"Maybe someday, when this is all behind me," I told DB, "I'll be able to write one of those dark comedies. I read something about comedians—that the great ones are actually very deep, tortured people who use their comedy as a form of therapy. I can believe it too. That's another funny thing about Dick and Bianca: neither one had any sense of humor."

I chugged the rest of my beer and ate some nuts.

CHAPTER 4

D B leaned forward again, chewed her bottom lip, and put her pad down. "Violet, I hope you don't mind me back-tracking a little, and I hope the subject doesn't upset you too much."

"Go ahead, ask whatever you want."

"Your father's dirty business made me think of what happened about four years ago, back in the spring of 1980, at the high school—the murders. Do you remember them?"

"Sure I do. I was only a sophomore then, and I didn't really know any of them too well. Seniors are in a different universe, and footballers are huge—like grown men."

I tried to think back to that time—the two years since high school felt more like forty-two.

"I'm one of those people who doesn't think of high school as the best years of my life. I don't even know what 'best' means anyway. Most of the kids made my life miserable because I aced everything. I wasn't interested in boys either; most of them had bad skin and I couldn't stand their stink, their idiot laughter. The thought of cheerleading them on made me want to puke. I took some grief, but so did lots of other kids. It goes on in every town in every state—big or small. Kids are cruel, especially if you don't fit a mold. I just rolled with it and kept my head down. Hey, did you ever notice how people love movies where a load of teenagers die?"

"But how did the murders affect *you*?"

"I mean, I was as shocked as everybody else. I couldn't believe it. It was way beyond anything I could ever imagine. Lots of kids went for counseling after that, but I didn't. I wasn't sure what anybody could say to me that would make any difference. As bad as it was, I was kind of neutral about it. I didn't like any of them. Most of the teachers were lame too—especially one of the math teachers. A real old perv."

DB nodded solemnly. "Well, I bring it up because, frankly, many of the details were kept quiet. It looked like a contract job, maybe ordered by whatever mob makes and distributes child pornography—the kind it sounds like your stepfather favored. Most porn producers use adults who are thin and young looking enough to pass for adolescent or pre-adolescent, but these types recruit or kidnap kids."

She narrowed her eyes, as if weighing the benefits of going on; she must have deemed it worth something, because she continued.

"We didn't release what those four kids were up to. They were making homemade porn in the basements of their parents' houses. They distributed them—mailed them out to people who put their names on lists, as buyers. We found about a hundred VHS tapes in a padlocked footlocker—all of the four of them."

"Holy shit, that's gross."

The four kids' faces swam up from a murky bottom and broke the surface. Tiffani? I didn't really know her at all, but she'd say something bitchy to me once in a while. Stephanie sat in front of me in French class, was always playing with her hair, never turned around. Kenny, no real recollection, another dumb jock. Demo had been in my Geometry class, even dumber than Kenny. I remembered something—"Demo showed up one morning all beat up and limping. I thought he got in a fight, and I didn't much care. He probably deserved it. They all started to look the same to me—just a bunch of pimply dicks or mean girls with fake noses. You know, the usual."

DB said she'd always suspected they were targeted because they wouldn't give the ring a hefty piece of the action, and if that was true, then it was a big mistake.

"Ugly thing for kids to be involved in, but not unique," she summarized ruefully. "That's not my end of things, but it did factor into my investigation. The tapes were turned over to vice. The kids all came from good homes, plenty of money. It didn't make sense, what they were into, but lots of things don't these days. I only bring this up because of what your stepfather was into. I have no idea whether it ties in or not. I just wonder if you ever heard anything—phone conversations, anything else. We've got people working their way through your stepfather's stash to see if any of them are the ones your schoolmates produced—whether he, in fact, might have produced any. We know he put ads in several papers looking for actors."

I showed no reaction, told her I wasn't surprised by anything they found out about Dick. But Khalika had already told me about those tapes. She found them in Dick's stash. She said she had a great time reviewing them, freeze-framing their faces at key moments, during or right after the money shots. She laughed herself sick at the two jocks' asses going up and down in closeups, where you could even see the pimples. She left one in a dressing room somewhere, just to see what would happen. But before the crap hit the air conditioner, they were all dead.

"They couldn't act for shit either," Khalika added—always the critic. "And they needed a better lighting director."

Khali thought they were all addicted to the easy money, the best drugs. They didn't think about the future, about their families. They were greedy and dumb. They started showing up in $100 sneakers that their parents probably never questioned. Maybe the parents were making their own homemade sin or inviting the neighbors in. Not long after that, the dream was over. Khalika even entertained the idea that one or more of the parents of the fab four arranged the hits on Dick and Bianca. You know, got together and pooled their money?

"Those jocks and their girlfriends? They sure were a bad

investment, weren't they?" Khalika said, laughing that deep whiskey laugh. "Hardly worth the labor pains and stretching the old yoni."

What I told DB was: "Dick said he bet their parents were glad they didn't have to pay for college or weddings. Standard stuff."

That pretty much ended the interview. She handed me her card and asked me to call her if I thought of anything else. I said I surely would.

"And Violet, if you need somebody to talk to, I'm always available. My home number is on the back. Call any time. Let me know if you remember anything else."

Before she reached the door, she turned to me.

"By the way, give me a call when you sort out where you're going. The house is still a crime scene for now. And don't be surprised, given Dick's activities, if Manhattan Vice contacts you somewhere down the line."

I said I would, added that I'd never set foot in the house again, even if I could.

DB paused at the door, an inscrutable look on her face. She cleared her throat before proceeding.

"I wonder, Violet, why you never reported your stepfather, even after you knew what he was doing. Were you afraid?"

I didn't hesitate.

"Nope, nothing like that. I was scared I'd lose Mercutio. He's the only reason I ever stuck around that hellhole."

CHAPTER 5

The barn had long been a kind of alternate reality for us, a benign one. After Mercutio arrived, Khalika and I hung out there more and more. Sometimes, after I'd ridden Mercutio on the trails that ran through the estate, brushed him out, and fed him, we'd talk about what we'd do when we got out of there, how we could make enough to live on before our inheritance came through. Only the moon, stars, Mercutio, and the slate-gray cat, Nimrod, heard our whispered conspiracies.

We adopted Nimrod after he wandered into the barn one night, a tiny gray dust moat who immediately befriended Mercutio. I found him curled up in the corner of his stall and for a few weeks I fed him formula with an eyedropper as Merc looked on in approval. Nimrod had no taste for mice—thus, the ironic name. One could scamper right in front of him and he'd just watch it with great curiosity. I had to rub his butt with a rough towel twice a day to make him pee. He never did get very big, but he sure took to Mercutio. And vice-versa.

When we were younger, we'd walk a lot—all over, whether it was hot or cold—often through the weeds and down to a lake near the house. Sometimes Khalika would walk with me for a while, then remember something she needed to do. She'd just say something like, "Later—stay awake, dummy," and walk off, all loose-limbed and snaky.

Sometimes, after she'd split pretty much for good, I'd head off the property, take trains and buses to find new places to explore. I'd eat lunch in funky little diners or from carts. No one cared what I did. Once I even walked on the narrow concrete ledge of an overpass over a major road, traffic whizzing by below. I felt high when I made it to the end of the ledge, laughed hysterically. But I never stopped missing her company. I could feel her presence, as if she might pop up from behind a bush any second and tell me about her latest money-making scheme. She would have been mad at me if she knew about my overpass caper. "You trying to check out early Vi? Don't fucking do that again!"

What's the diagnosis when you are hot to live but drawn to extinction, when there are days when it's hard to choose? I'm sure all the experts have opinions.

"Screw the experts," Khalika said, "before they screw you. Besides, everybody thinks those kinds of things. It's part of this existence deal. No way to feel just one way about it. The ones who claim they do are lying."

Around the time I turned thirteen, Dick started being nicer to me, working himself up to messing with me. Somehow, I'd always expected it would happen. He'd sneak up behind my chair and blow his cigar breath on my cheek or play with my hair. I'd feel the puke rise in my throat before I shrugged him off.

That phase didn't last long, though. When I told Khalika what was going on, she just smiled and said, "Leave it to me." After she had a word with him; he never laid a hand on me again, hardly even looked at me. I don't know what she said to him, but it sure scared him. That wasn't the first time Khalika protected me from a predator, though—an outside one.

Not long after, in the summer of '78, something happened. And from that point on, I became hyper-alert to everything going on around me, like a gazelle on the Serengeti.

The season was winding down; Khalika met me at the end of one of my marathon walks and we snuck in the side door of an art house that specialized in resurrecting old films. We both scooted down in the balcony seats to watch a French film that featured some tasteful nudity.

After it was over, Khalika directed me to go up to the ticket window and pay the admission price for both of us.

The lady looked really confused when I shoved the money through the opening, said dinner and drinks were on us.

"Gotta do our part to keep the place open!" Khalika yelled over her shoulder, laughing as we ran off. Khalika hated buses, the lurching, the crazies who traveled on them. She said she'd meet me back at the barn in a couple of hours.

CHAPTER 6

So, this is how it happened—the first time I realized that when you're out in the world, you're never really alone for long. Sooner or later, there'll be at least one pair of eyes on you. Sometimes, the beast won't be hungry; maybe it had just eaten or come off sex or something else that might make it pass you by. When it was hungry, though, I got to where I could sense it, like an animal that hasn't entirely lost its survival instincts.

You might call it a gut feeling, but not me. My spine tells me.

Everything changed for me too after Dollar Man. I can't really remember exactly why. The details, except for his actual appearance that day, stayed fuzzy even after we'd written it out together as a story, stored it in the boxes with the others.

EXT. A street somewhere on the outskirts of Westchester, New York. June 1978.

A girl walks to the bus stop after a movie. She's distracted, daydreaming, looking down at the cracks in the pavement. "Riders on the Storm" by Jim Morrison plays in the background.

Camera slowly pans out over area, until all the people appear small, insignificant in relation to the hunting ground. Camera pans in again, so that only the girl is in the frame.

NARRATOR (V.O.)
The sun is just sinking when Dollar
Man seems to materialize out of thin
air. He is parked at the curb in an
early model, beat-up car, the color
of sludge. My stepfather's sickness is
familiar to me, as it was even before
then. I believe I am inured to it, that
it has become background noise to anything else that's going on around me.

Camera pans out again and follows the girl who,
it is now clear, is the narrator, as she sits
on a bench at the bus stop.

NARRATOR (V.O.) (CON'T)
My sister, of course, could never accept this — that I remained in that
house, with Dick and Bianca, and she
has worked on me tirelessly to get me
to see it her way.

"That's why crazy parents get away with
so much for so long," she insists. "The
kids are scared to tell, afraid to lose
what they have, get stuck with something even worse. It's the devils you
know."

I tell her that I know all this, but
that it's not time yet.

"Besides, how often are we even there?"

Dollar Man is different though, an ap-

parition that I conjure from a future
that is already upon me, or, as I come
to understand, one that existed forever, stretching into the black abysm of
time, that curled itself around that
future like a boa constrictor consuming
its own tail.

Camera shifts to a view of apartments lining the
street, stops at one of the lower windows in the
development.

        NARRATOR (V.O.) (CON'T)
I am preoccupied, thinking of the movie, wondering if the bus will be on
time. I look at the run-down and sinking apartments that line the sidewalk,
an alien world compared to where I've
grown up. I imagine what might go on
behind the dirty windows, a dull misery
that plays out in the rooms of these
sectioned warrens. They simmer over a
low flame until, one day, one evening,
in one of them, the lid blows off.

Once, on another walk, I thought I
saw a girl, pale and still as a mannequin, staring out at me from one
of those windows, before she quickly
turned away. They're all the same, I
think, whether the lawns are manicured
or weed-choked. Then, beyond them, the
streets — litter-strewn or carefully swept. Nobody would think too much
about what might be in the weeds around

the lakes where power boats speed by
summer picnics. You had to make a living, no matter what, to buy the fixings
for those sunny memories. Without money
you are nothing — less than nothing.
You may not even be fit for consumption;
they're glutted on the pickings, sated
yet still ravenous. Wrap it up, maybe
I'll be hungry later. That must have
been what Dick and Bianca decided, way
back, before they became vampires. You
can never get enough. The trough still
overflows here. Keep eating.

Camera focuses in for a choker shot of the girl.

                    NARRATOR (V.O.) (CON'T)
I am looking down as I approach a
parked car, but something makes me
look up, that signal, an alarm going
off in my back, like those old school
fire drills. I take him in all at once,
sitting there in his car, still as a
waxwork and holding something above
the steering wheel, between a skeletal
thumb and forefinger.

It is a silver dollar. I can tell by
the size of it as the dying sun bounc-
es off it. He rotates it slowly — in
a small arc. He is otherwise frozen,
another mannequin, a body in a morgue
sitting upright. The signal says,
"Heads up, dummy!" The hairs stand up
on my arms, the back of my neck. I feel

a shiver, even though it is quite warm,
and still.

The seated dummy is the color of ash,
and the sun reflects off his glasses as
well, so he looks like somebody in a
Little Orphan Annie cartoon — the one
where Annie is never seen again.

It's hypnotic the way he manipulates
the coin, the way it flashes in coun-
terpoint to the opaque whiteness of
his glasses. He is smiling — the silver plate on a coffin . . . Then, stand-
ing there, glued to the sidewalk, I get
this flash, like, if I don't run, and
fast, I'll never be seen alive again.
And who would miss me besides my sister, my horse, and his cat?

Camera pans out again to the surrounding,
as-yet-undeveloped landscape.

> NARRATOR (V.O.) (CON'T)
> Until one day . . . somebody — a bird
> watcher maybe, a kid playing hide-and-
> seek — stumbles over something soft in
> the woods, something giving way under-
> foot. Or they smell something so inde-
> scribably awful, they'll never be able
> to wipe it from the slate of memory or
> describe it. And they run, almost stum-
> bling in their panic to flee whatever
> lay there, obscured by debris and veg-
> etation, what might be about to swim
> into their vision.

If it does, they will see her splayed
and propped in lurid display, her
mouth twisted in final agony or slightly rounded, like a child's about to
mouth its first word . . . ma . . .
ma . . .

I wouldn't have been able to describe
it then, but almost a decade later,
I see I must have known that you had
only a moment — maybe less than that —
and that it must have always been this
way. That to pretend it wasn't would
make you disappear, like a small star
that had been sucked into the event
horizon. Dick and Bianca's event horizon. It can't get enough of you . . .
you Nordic goddess, you backwoods
beauty queen, you unlucky boulevard
runaway fresh off the bus.

Whatever future, unreeling behind your
back, would be snapped up, crunched
down, its light extinguished.

Before I start to rot, he's long gone
in his stained, litter-strewn shit
wagon, maybe with me in the trunk.
He guns the engine, drives down the
road with one pale arm stuck out the
window, sitting in a vinyl seat that
smells of his ass, his grinning pocky
face. Maybe he just leaves me where he
sliced or choked me, revisits me later to fuck death. Yeah, I came back,

put lipstick on her, propped her up
against a tree. I was so hard . . .
harder even than when I saw my mother
with the guy she brought home and took
him in . . . all the way in, until she
gagged and he laughed.

Even if you could somehow exterminate
them all, a new crop would be gestat-
ing in their proud, celebrating mothers, or spring up from where they lay
dead — spore brought in by an alien
mothership.

You'd need to get them before they
were ever born. All of them — the
Dicks and the Biancas. Every last one
of them.

Camera follows the girl, close up, like a predator about to pounce.

          NARRATOR (V.O.) (CON'T)
I run then, as if he might drop down
on me like a hawk on a mouse. I run
until I get to the next bus stop,
crouch down until I get my breath.

Fade to black.
END scene.

Internal dialog in this one, even if some directors hate that.
When you write your own scene, you can bend the rules as
much as you want. I like to let one scene bleed into another.

Don't let the audience catch its breath. That's the way to hook them.

Khalika stayed away for a long time after we wrote it out. Then came the asshole's failed attempt to get a shrink to adjust her attitude. And after that, she more or less cleared out for real; the events having seriously fucked with her equilibrium. As for me, I, as usual, just filed it all away somewhere, out of sight, out of reach. On the rare occasions she did appear, she'd tell me she'd been crashing with friends. At fourteen or so, she started fencing stolen goods, dealing pot, other stuff. She said not to worry—she knew what she was doing. *Khalika of the icy stare, of the iron-rod spine.*

Most people don't think too much about what's out there. They shove it into the dank basement in their heads until the day it pops up like a jack-in-the-box they accidentally trip over and activate. The thing is, there's a gazillion replicas of Dollar Man out there—the twisted fucker in his pit-stained polyester shirt, holding up the shiny thing—a cop's badge, a puppy, a kitten, a sob story of good lovin' gone bad. There's a million Dicks and Biancas out there too—planning, plotting, screaming, fighting over credit cards or who to fuck, or fuck over, next.

Fast forward a few years and there's more and more of them—grinning at you from across the room, the subway aisle, the factory, the conference table. They're leaning against a tree outside the school yard, watching you from behind a bush as you bend to collect a rock, a coin. He's behind you at the theatre, a rock concert, an upscale bar, backstage at the Metropolitan. They're the Dicks, grinning at you across a huge teak desk, imagining what's going to be done to you. They find you stuffed in a heating duct, most of the bones in your lower extremities shattered.

Whatever. The floodgates have opened now—props to cars. And you thought they only fucked up the air? Anybody can buy one on the installment plan with zero down. You get a steady diet of it on the news, so it's just background noise, like the open-air porn bins on Broadway, like what Dick and Bianca were up to in JeanLuc and Oceane's former home—a masterpiece out of *Architectural Digest* tainted by their filth and, now, infected molecules of their remains.

It's just the way it is now, like it always was, I suppose— but so much easier, even for the really stupid ones. It's up there in your face, in your shit. Hey, if you can't get over it, let it seep into your day-to-day, like pus through a bandage, then put in a transfer to a better planet—one with a God that doesn't come down and fuck married virgins, then nail up the result. One where everything doesn't eat everything in its path.

Khalika says let them pay for their own goddamned sins, in the fucking here and now. Let *them* bleed. Bleed out on Highway 61.

CHAPTER 7

July 1984

During her interview, DB had asked whether I'd over-heard anything that could be significant—calls or discussions about threats. I'd told her no, but that wasn't true. What else is new?

Two weeks before the murders, Khalika was at the Westchester house. She showed up one afternoon, told me to lay low, suggested I tack up Merc and go for a ride. This time, she said, she wasn't there just to see me; she planned on lifting some cash from Dick's wallet. He never missed a couple of hundreds, she said.

Dick was infuriated whenever she blew in. He showed it by clamming up, his jaw muscles bunching, tanned face going livid with rage. He hated her way more than he did me.

There was no way around her.

Dick decided to come home for dinner that night and soon enough, the phone rang. Khalika listened in. She didn't have to listen very long to know it was about another late payment to his partners. Lately, they were getting more and more in arrears, but this time it was over two months overdue. The caller said he needed to talk to him and to meet him at the Naked Envy—the den of iniquity I mentioned somewhere back there—at 9:30 p.m. Before Dick could ask who to look for, the caller slammed the receiver down. After that, Dick was in a fouler mood than usual, and Bianca started needling him. She knew how to get under his thin skin. She had worked him into a frenzy before he summoned the chauffeur and stomped out again, snarling, around 8:30.

Naked Envy is a strip bar and smurfing front on 53rd and Lexington. Dick owned part of it, and it was one of his favorite hangouts. He loved the player image, but that night he was having trouble pulling it off—the Don Johnson vibe, I mean. I know this, because—not for the first time—Khalika got to the Envy before Dick and waited for him to show. Dick might have been pretty dumb and totally lacking in imagination, but his instincts were as savage as one of Anne Rice's lower-IQ blood drinkers. One such as Khalika—or me, for that matter—could never have shot out of that ball sac.

When I asked Khalika once why she'd want to go there so often, all she told me was that she was just "getting the lay of the land and picking up some good dialogue." And that was it. As usual, I would be enlightened further when she was damn good and ready.

Khalika—of the platinum blond cornrow wig, huge sunglasses, and wide-brimmed hat—wandered through the doors of the Envy after Dick and sat down to his right. Once he noticed her, he swiveled around and tried to strike up a conversation, even though Khalika, being pretty tall and well built, looked way older than twelve, Dick's preferred age group. Khalika, under her hat, didn't look at him.

Anybody who frequents these places knows the dancers aren't permitted to sit and chat with customers—and that goes for any woman who wanders in too. Vice might show up at any time. Nobody wanted them to get the idea that prostitution might be going on in there.

Insert eye roll.

Khalika cut him off quickly. "I'm here for a job, not a date."

But Dick, being Dick, tried again.

"I don't want one. I own the place." He thought a moment, then: "You're not even my type. Can you dance? And what's with the sunglasses and the hat? Afraid somebody's gonna ask for your autograph?"

Khalika, without looking up, told him to please go beat off somewhere, as she had just had a miscarriage on the bathroom floor at a convenience store. He made a gagging noise, but that shut him up. He hated to hear of pussy being utilized for purposes other than those he had in mind, and he swiveled away from her in disgust, turning his attention back to the six-foot, trans stripper on the platform above the bar—Sue Nami—Amazon queen and comedian.

Nobody knew that Suzi once had a dick of her own. The customers were crazy about her. I knew she was once a he, because she told me one day in the back after I started dancing there—whoops, "spoiler alert!"—like it was the best joke ever. In her off hours, Suzi specialized in sadism. You might be surprised how many men pay big bucks to wind up in the ER. Or maybe you wouldn't. Suzi didn't do anything for free though, even if she enjoyed it. Nobody cared what the girls did outside the bar, except that they couldn't let it show on their faces or bodies. Then they'd dump you like a bad habit.

Next thing, the hulk Dick was talking to on the phone—presumably—materialized and sat down on Dick's left and ordered a top-shelf scotch and soda, watching the barmaid to make sure she didn't stint. Suzi punched in the songs she liked and walked down the bar to start her set, hung her kimono on a hook and walked up the steps. Her spangled G-string, silver and black, matched her pasties.

Khalika watched as Suzi started her set. First up was "Those Shoes" by the Eagles. Suzi climbed up and pretended to inspect her own sky-high shoes, smiling, shaking her head, shrugging her shoulders, palms up. Like I said, she was quite a comedian—all six-and-a-half feet of her. She told me once she only danced to add new clients to her roster. She couldn't get enough of hurting them, claimed she'd be able to retire before forty and move to someplace tropical. Lots of her clients were the movers and shakers you'd read about in the society pages, Wall Streeters flush with insider trading loot, underworld goons, even a cop or two. These places are just microcosms, after all, like Genet's universal brothel. The French word for brothel is "house of illusion." Nobody says it like the French, which is why Khalika and I have practically OD'd on French *nouvelle vague* films.

Anyway, Suzi didn't seem fazed by anything, and she was flexible too. She could stand on one foot in those shoes and pull the other leg over her head and do a stomach flutter. After the first number ended, Suzi turned to the mirrored wall, bent over until her hair mopped the stage and stuck her tongue out from between her calves. She turned around, sat back on her elbows, and scissored her legs open and closed. A thin, neat line of pubic hair was visible on either side of her G-string.

Dick took it all in, kind of bored, not noticing the time. Her big, high silicone fun bags were anything but pre-pubescent. Suzi licked her lips and flicked her tongue like a venomous snake before sticking her index finger in her glossy mouth and sucking on it.

Dick fiddled with his drink, flicked his ash, and continued to stare dully at Suzi until finally the hulk leaned in and said, all casual, "Hey Dickie boy, sorry to sneak up on you like this, but you looked like you were deep in thought, or deep in something. Thanks for being on time though. I hate to be kept waiting, even with entertainment."

Dick turned to him, startled. He didn't seem to recognize the guy, so Khalika figured he was expecting someone else. This one looked serious as a stroke, yet also kind of affable—in an amiable lunatic kind of way.

"I'm Ryker."

He offered his hand, but Dick declined, sneered. That was Dick's first mistake. Ryker gazed into Suzi's open thighs and gave a review: "Sometimes I like to see little muff, ya know? Give me a landing strip. These bald ones—I dunno—they make me think I'm fuckin' a mannequin, or maybe an android? And give me real tits every time—that jiggle, that sway. This one hasn't got any cellulite though. Real dancers, the ones from ballet or Broadway, hardly ever do. Anyway, that's a big girl there. She must have eaten her Wheaties."

The guy did a whole monologue, Khalika said, before Dick could manage a response.

"I do fine, thanks, but whatever stiffens your resolve, buddy."

Khalika said she could tell that Dick was starting to sweat a little.

Ryker flicked up his genial mask, revealing his business one, his expression hardening to granite.

"Personally, I like to cut all the lights and pretend I'm puttin' the stones to your bony-ass wife. You know, Dicky, you should shake hands when a guy offers. Bad manners don't get you very far in life. Any sleazy salesman knows that much."

Ryker sipped his scotch, debated with himself for a moment.

"Wait, I take that back. It's not that bony, considering she sits on it all day—except when she, uh, goes to lunch with the girls. I'm not telling you anything new, am I Dicky?"

Under her big hat, Khalika lit a cigarette and pretended to check out Sue Nami. Khalika had one thing in common with Dick: her smile never reached her eyes.

CHAPTER 8

Dick swiveled his head and stared at Ryker, outraged, his mouth slack. Suzi became more animated, trying to get their attention. Bills were already falling out of her crotch. She'd empty it at the end of her set. *Ka-ching!* Once, a twenty fell into the toilet in back, and she just let it go. "Maybe it'll reach somebody who needs it." She twirled her ankles in the air. Her stilettos had ankle straps made of thin silver chainmail. Another guy came up, passed her a $10.

Dick gave the tipper a dirty look before addressing Ryker.

"What the fuck did you just say? You wanna get bounced the fuck out of here?"

Ryker ratcheted up the menace a notch.

"You don't want to do anything like that. I suggest you calm the fuck down before I put you on the floor in front of this pretty girl."

Ryker jerked his thumb at Khalika, who snorted. The guy didn't seem to be worried about the bouncer.

"Pardon my French, sweetheart."

"No praa-blem," Khalika shot back, doing her perfect Marlene Dietrich imitation.

Ryker gave a thumbs up before turning his attention back to Dick. Dick got more submissive after that, and Ryker, nostalgic now, returned to reminiscing.

"Good boy. I used to close my eyes and dream I was doin' the old horizontal with Marcheline, my high school girlfriend, but lately it's mostly your little helpmeet. Variety is the spice and all."

Ryker really seemed to enjoy his work, and Khalika was digging it to the max.

"Does the old ball 'n' chain sport a Yul to keep up with the latest style in twats, or has the pie been off limits since before this song was a hit?"

Dick put both hands around his glass and festered.

"OK, enough. I told you I'd get the money. I always do."

Suzi adjusted her black fringed G-string before "Magic Bus" began its intro. Her pelvis was at eye level with all their faces, and she humped and ground the air before drawing her open legs almost behind her ears. She started to pull aside the crotch of her G-string, then aborted the move. Ryker grinned.

"I guess this would be where the camera cuts away if they want the R-rating."

He winked at Suzi and she smiled back at him. Ryker passed her a $50.

Suzi flipped over on her knees, did some more grinding.

"Ooof baby, I can almost see your breakfast."

Suzi sat up, folded the crisp bill lengthwise, snapped it between her manicured fingers, eyes fixed on the thug. She licked her lips, then slipped the bill into one of the chainmail straps on her shoe and blew him a kiss, her eyes hard and black as obsidian.

"Ever wonder where your paper money's been, Dicky? Maybe it's time they got rid of it, but then what would these little ladies do for shits and giggles?"

He leaned in even closer to whisper.

"Consider this your final warning, fuckwad. My employers? They got very little sense of fair play, and what they do have is draining away like pus from an infected sore on your dick. Now, I, or one of my associates, is gonna be here tomorrow night at 9:30 p.m. Be here with the full wad, plus interest. And I mean the *full* wad, no more consideration. Capiche?"

He drew back, smiled again, and backhanded Dick's cheek hard enough to make him jerk. Customers around the bar looked up, muttered to one another, turned back to Suzi and their drinks.

"No way I can get it by tomorrow. Tell them I need another week, tops."

Now Dick was sweating for real.

"Nope, you've already had two, and that's two too many, hotshot. Be here with the money's all I'm sayin'—9:30. Don't be late."

Ryker smiled, downed his second scotch in one go, and spun around on his stool. Suzi was ending her set, and he saluted her. She smiled down at him like a Mayan priestess who'd just eaten the heart of a sacrificed infant. Suzi was the future, Khalika decided—the embodiment of it practically, the prototype.

Over his shoulder, Ryker said genially, "Meantime, don't hide the salami anywhere I wouldn't."

The next offering mounted the steps to the platform. Snowy Peaks, thin and startled under the spotlight—like a filly at the Kentucky yearling sales. Just Dick's type, like she fell off the hay truck and needed a sandwich. When the music started, she tried too hard. Dancing in these places, you've got to look like you wouldn't piss on any of them if they were going up in flames. It's best when you're unapproachable; if you smile, you've got to look like it's because you want to eat their organs raw. In these places, sex is wound up with violence, like maybe it is everywhere. Once in a while, though, you'll get a bozo who likes them to look all innocent and vulnerable, so they can play Daddy, or worse.

That would be Dick.

Khalika thinks it's hardwired in their brains—the need to humiliate, to be humiliated, or maybe it's something Mom or Dad did, behind those weed-choked or manicured lawns.

"But for some, it's the chase, subduing, bringing down of prey, that's everything," she said, later that night. "It's all scrambled up in there, from when they first slide into the world and discover that they call the shots, even if they're dog-shit stupid. Lots of women go for the best predators too. They want to breed with them to continue the line, to make sure there's a steady supply of world beaters." She stared into the darkness for a moment.

"Of course, there is that rare breed of female that indulges her thrill of the chase. It's called poaching."

Dick stared after the thug, still rubbing his cheek, then pretended to turn his attention back to the dancer. The new girl had gotten down on the floor and swung her body around so that she was on her knees, facing the mirrored wall. She gyrated her ass in Dick's face, mimicking Suzi, then looked behind her, trying out her best smirk. Her beaded, pink-and-blue G-string featured a Minnie Mouse motif, and there were a couple of singles and fives hanging out of it, fore and aft, Khalika reported.

"Give her a few weeks, and she'll be grinding in their stupid faces with the best of them."

With that, Khalika treated me to one of her famous impromptu scenes:

INT. Naked Envy, evening. July 1984. Cue "Sharp Dressed Man" by ZZ Top.

A man — Dick Danzinger, who viewers may know from *An Asshole out of Hell* — leaps over the bar, up onto the stage. He drops to his knees and, before she knows what's happening, bites the skinny dancer's rear savagely before reaching into his unstructured jacket for a hunting knife and disemboweling her, spraying the zombified clot of humanoids lining the bar with a fire hose of blood.

He fishes around in the gore, picks up her

entrails and flings them — raw scraps to jackals
— and laughs like a jackhammer. He extracts a
gold monogrammed cigarette case from his jacket,
takes one out, taps it on the case a few times
before jumping down and lighting it nonchalantly in the aisle. He is soaked in the dancer's
blood.

Grinning grotesquely, like the master of cere-
monies from *Cabaret*, Dick does a jaunty, Broad-
way-style kick-walk toward the exit in time to
the music. The onlookers, now fully animated,
stuff their maws with the gore he's tossed, fight
over it — a feeding frenzy.

Freeze frame closeup on Dick's bloody face. Dick
winks at the camera, does jazz hands as he exits
into the anonymity of the Manhattan night.

END scene.

I applauded enthusiastically. "Too funny!"

Khalika enjoyed creating these scenes, executing the mental gymnastics, sticking the dismount. A perfect ten on this
one, as usual. Short and sweet, yet full of visual knockouts.
These exercises helped diffuse the rage, she admitted, gave her
ideas for our future endeavors. As for me, I liked to think they
helped me understand things better, but in reality, I think it
felt better to imagine everything in digestible chunks, from a
distance. So that's how she fed it to me.

"Don't fret, little sister; they're both in the dirt now. Hoist
on their own petards, and O, 'tis most sweet when in one line
two crafts directly meet." Khalika saluted skyward. "All props
to the Bard of Warwickshire!"

Khalika winked, made a sweeping stage bow to an imaginary Shakespeare, then drew her index finger across her
throat.

"They would have killed that dude if they knew what he was up to—a real subversive, that one, playing cat-and-mouse with King James—the wisest fool in Christendom."

But back to the action:

Of course, Dick just sat there massaging his face, and Khalika laughed silently at his obvious humiliation. He collected himself, rubbed one finger on top of the other in the "naughty" gesture, and downed his drink. He signaled the barmaid to pour him another double, which he flung down. He passed a crisp hundred, along with his card, to the neophyte, and her eyes popped before she tucked them both into her G-string, front and center.

"It was like she snagged an Oscar," Khalika told me, laughing.

Dick stood up and slapped a tip on the bar, headed off to the back for a piss. Khalika exited, lit a cigarette in the vestibule, and listened to Ryker on the pay phone.

Ryker didn't bother to turn around. He didn't care who heard him.

"Uh-huh, he's lookin' for another week . . . I know. I'm thinkin' we need to maybe let him know how serious this is. He plays fast and loose, and I think he's into something worse than we know about, and when I say bad . . . uh-huh . . . yeah, that bad. He's got more stuff than cash. Yeah, yeah . . . uh-huh, sure. Just let me know what you wanna do, and I'll organize it. Blackmail won't fly, 'cause the wife hates him. Maybe she's already filed but hasn't served him yet. On the other hand, she's probably in it with him up to her fake tits. Sheesh, what an asshole. I'd beat the snot out of him for free, no shit," he said, and chuckled.

Khalika didn't need to hear more. She headed back to paradise to drop off the script.

CHAPTER 9

August 1984

In the barn, Khali and I listened to Malfitano ace the last act of *Madama Butterfly—Morte di Butterfly*—on the boombox. We both appreciated opera, but it had to be kick-ass, the very best. I mean, it's always the same plot, where the soprano suffers and dies for shit never caused. I don't even consider Carmen to be a villain, except in the eyes of man. She was just before her time, like Khalika is. The final scene is killer, of course. They all are. All props to Puccini. Even Merc and Nimmy, perched on his back, seemed impressed. The bought bride disembowels herself right before the sperm donor shows up with his new white wife to claim the kid. Khalika said she was a real toe rag if she stayed with Pinkerton after that.

Khalika insisted that when these guys came to lay a beating on Dick, I should be in the barn, hiding in the hayloft. I'd know because Mercutio would know, would start snorting and pacing, and crazy Nimrod would jump down on his back from the rafters to calm him. I used to wonder who owned who in that relationship.

"No music for a few days," she warned. "And no lights! It won't be long now, because we both know Dick is broke, that this dump is mortgaged to the hilt, *and* he's borrowed even more from some very unsavory types."

I told her she better not fuck off on me again, that I couldn't get through this without her. She reassured me that she would be around until it happened, and I believed her. She seemed to live for this stuff. Her pupils were dilated like she'd taken a hit of something stronger than beer.

"I'm just high on life," she joked.

"Hey, if the prick is broke, what happens to Mercutio?"

"I said you needed to trust me" was all she would say.

A couple of weeks after Ryker's warning to Dick, Khalika returned to the Envy to ask about a job. She spoke to the manager, a big, stupid oaf straining the seams of his shiny suit. She opened her coat and showed him the merchandise. She wore a black one-piece made basically of strings—a spider's web—and thigh-high red boots. He asked if she was legal and she said she was, had already been dancing across the river in Jersey before she realized Manhattan was more lucrative. Lurch said auditions were the first Monday of every month. Khalika put her name on the list on my behalf.

"You're the dancer, and besides, you'll need the money," she said by way of explanation. "I don't want you mixed up in what I'm doing." She told me I'd find out soon enough about her reasons for getting me the gig at the Envy.

"Don't tell me I'm a plant now!"

Khalika just smiled, lit a cigarette. "You'll just have to trust me on this one too. It'll be good exercise—mental *and* physical, if it wasn't for those feet-mangling shoes."

Khalika also wanted me to test out the getup she wore to travel on the train, said it was genius. All her hair under a cap, no makeup. Baggy jeans and a work shirt. The first time she wore it, a passing punk looked her up and down and hissed, "Fucking faggot." She didn't even flinch, just pulled up her T-shirt and flashed him. That shut him up. Another time, a transvestite in full stage makeup, wearing platforms and trailing parrot plumage, checked her out, trying to decide if she was mid-transition.

Khalika told me she was preparing me for making a living off the radar, like she did, until our inheritance came through. She predicted that Dick would get more and more desperate as the money ran out—got pissed away.

"Stupid, desperate Dicks do stupid, desperate things."

Khalika suggested we hang out around 47th and Broadway for a while, get a feel for the environment. She'd lied about working in Jersey, but she had used a fake ID to get barmaid jobs in a few clubs there for a while.

"I'm gonna bring you out of the shadows," Khalika assured me. "You will transition from a shrinking violet to an ultra, break free from your chrysalis."

I had to agree that I was developing a knack for navigating the deepest, most polluted waters, for choosing another, less open face from the ancient gallery, as Jim Morrison put it, and running with it.

"It's about time," she laughed.

CHAPTER 10

On August 24, 1984, Khalika showed up at the house at dinnertime a few days after our last trip into Manhattan, where we'd ridden the subways all over, in the wee hours.

The four of us sat at the long table in the formal dining room, served by the housekeeper, Lupe.

Even when she'd lived there, my sister almost never ate at that table, except when she decided I needed her support. No matter how she goaded them, neither Dick nor Bianca would spar with her. They knew, she said, that she had the goods on them and wouldn't hesitate to spill, if necessary, whenever and to whomever she pleased. She wanted me to learn to fight back, to make them fear me as much as they did her. But I'd been frozen for so long, beaten down. As much as I hated my stepparents, I couldn't bring myself to rock the leaky, rotting boat.

Lupe had been nervous around Khalika since our teenage years, even before that—her black clothes, the weird jewelry, punk down to the ground. Whenever Khalika showed up, she'd loot the fridge, lift cash. Jewelry would disappear. Lupe got blamed at first, even though they knew she would never steal. She was very religious—a practicing Catholic. Lupe often saw or heard things in the Westchester house that made her quickly cross herself, cluck her tongue. I think Lupe wanted to quit, but she stayed on for the money. She had four kids to support, and her ex had run off with the upstairs neighbor, who wound up stabbing him to death.

Anyway, on this night, Khalika sat slumped at the table—not eating, just glaring—her eyes burning holes in their stupid, smug faces. Dick and Bianca wouldn't look at her, kept eating and swilling their expensive frog water.

Khalika told Lupe, still staring at them, that she didn't need a plate. I wasn't hungry either; I picked at what Lupe had prepared. Khalika, winking at me, suddenly rose from her chair, a warning blast of steam from a volcano tuning up to blow its lid. She walked slowly around to Dick's side, bending over him.

"Enjoy your unborn lamb, you jumped-up mother fucker."

Dick didn't react, but his face was a mottled crimson that spread up from his shirt collar, showed through his tan.

Khalika, smiling horribly, moved on behind Bianca's chair, whispered, "Some prize you got there, Lady MacB. Enjoy your fabulous, useless life here in my parents' former home. See you in the next world, whore—maybe—don't be late."

Khalika looked over at me for a moment, and I almost smiled at her Jimi Hendrix—"Voodoo Child"—reference, but I resisted.

She exited the dining room in long, silent strides before curling around the corner like smoke. I didn't even hear the front door open or close. Khalika was quiet as a vampire, and just as seductive.

That night, the world blew up again. Dick didn't get beaten up after all. He got dead, along with his accomplice. If I hadn't stayed in the barn, I likely would have been slaughtered as well. Raped, maybe, and sliced to ribbons in an architectural wonder on a hundred acres of fucking paradise.

I don't know how she knew they were coming that night. But there's lots of things nobody—not even me—will ever understand about Khalika. And if you haven't figured it out yet, let me clue you in: she's a stone-cold fox and a bad mother . . . shut my mouth.

ACT II

What can an eternity of damnation matter to someone who has felt, if only for a second, the infinity of delight.

—Charles Baudelaire

CHAPTER 1

Sisters always want back after giving. They never give and leave.

—Jinzo

February 1985

I'd been living in my little loft for nearly half a year. The Westchester house, mortgaged to the hilt, was seized by the bank, along with truckloads of valuable shit. They got Jean-Luc's art. No will, because these types never expect to die. Others practically rehearse for it. The ones who don't leave all kinds of filth in their safes, in bank deposit boxes with the fenced jewelry and laundered cash. It's comical in a way—it's like they think they're immortal—like vampires. Khalika once said she was surprised that their images were reflected in mirrors.

The place would have been a hard sell anyway, because of the bloodbath. Of course, some freaks love to live in horror houses. In fact, they make shitloads of money telling stories of horny demons who want to fuck them in half after they get bored with chucking chairs and plates around. Why else would they buy it, even at a bargain price?

Khalika said she doesn't think there's anything you couldn't find somebody to buy, especially if they thought they could turn a profit. So sure, live happily ever after in a house with a killing floor. Even then, the aura of what happened would be inside the walls, the ceiling, the cupboards—crouching in the eaves. Dead birds would be found in the window wells. Waking up in the middle of the night, voices, everything off kilter. Khalika claims she felt it in the house from the start, then, whenever she was there. It was like an unresolved tension in the air, emanating from the bones of our parents' former home. I felt and saw it too, but I tried to push it away. The house stunk of the capital vices too—all seven of them—with exploitation and murder thrown in.

It really needed to be razed, we decided.

The crime scene: the cops had first dibs. The yellow tape went up. They confiscated all the underage stuff, some snuff porn that Khalika had already viewed and thought looked fake. There would only be one copy of the real deal—in the hands of the proud owner. I guess people want to believe only so much about this kind of thing and no more. Their psyches must reject to protect, until there's no denying it anymore—until it visits your block, your house. They'll read about it, shake their heads, and go on. It's all they can do. Maybe they want to believe that, if they are very careful, it will never touch them or theirs, will never reach out its clammy hand and grasp them from behind by the throat, take them down, down, down, past the basement of what can be assimilated by the mind.

After the bank's big grab, all I needed to do was pack my suitcases, Mercutio's tack, some clothes, my books and music, and a few boxes of odds and ends, mostly papers and photos. Dick's partners, the so-called legit ones, took over the agency. After all, they'd bankrolled it and had the biggest stake in it. Naked Envy went on as before, its sulfurous stench mixing with cigarette smoke and cigar butts, spilled beer, cheap or expensive aftershave and stale testosterone. I boarded Mercutio, and the girl who owned the barn agreed to feed his cat with her own as part of the deal. I couldn't separate them. Nimrod would have hated living in the loft anyway, as much as Mercutio would have, even if I could have shrunk him down and snuck him up there in a carrier. I promised Mercutio that I'd visit regularly, take him out for adventures on the surrounding acreage. I'm already saving for a trailer so we can explore other places. The barn owner said I could hitch it to her pickup any time I wanted. I keep my money—which is quite a stash already—in the dishwasher. They don't have a clue who

I am at the Envy—the stepdaughter of their dead partner.

Before we parted company for the last time, DB said to call her if I needed anything. I said I'd stay in touch. I was closing in on the big 2-0 and could legally be on my own. I was really flying, wasn't worried. I could handle it.

On a Monday afternoon not long after I signed the lease on the loft, I put the spider outfit on, took the subway to the Envy, and auditioned to Bob Dylan's "New Pony." It wasn't hard to nail it. The new pony went through the paces. The few years of dance lessons Dick paid for to keep me occupied really paid off. Thanks, Dick.

Lurch, the manager, remembered Khalika, of course, minus the blond cornrow wig and street talk this time. I had lots of good moves I'd picked up when Khalika and I had checked out a few belly-dance dives on 8th Avenue in the Village. We were entranced by these women whose movements reflected everything female. Some of the dancers looked over fifty. They hit on everything—sex, birth, death, grief, joy—to the ancient, dark throb of a doumbek, getting it on with the haunted strings of an oud. I couldn't get enough of it. They were like goddesses in the flesh, and in the dim light, hypnotic.

I was hired on the spot and Frank, the day bartender, penciled me into the schedule. Lurch had some kind of accent I couldn't place. Dollar signs flashed behind his blank, detached stare.

I walked out onto the street and started back to the train. After I'd walked a few blocks, I suddenly felt like I'd been dropped into a scene from *Freaks*. The buildings on either side of Lexington Avenue loomed huge and monolithic, nightmare structures out of scale with the frenzied humans skittering around under them like beetles, or puppets jerked wildly by a lunatic puppeteer on uppers. One argued with himself, slapped himself in the face. Another screamed threats at the sky, gesticulated, then leapt around in a circle in a strangely graceful frenzy before collapsing in a doorway, laughing maniacally. Farther on, a woman in a bathrobe and slippers hissed, "Dirty cunt," at me and stuck out her tongue, waggled it obscenely before using it to flick out her two front teeth. As I reached 5th Avenue, a Black guy in a Hawaiian shirt punched at an invisible assailant, gritting his teeth, drooling. "Motherfucker mess with me . . . come at me, bitch."

All this in the space of a few blocks. It was getting crazier out here by the day. "Just like home," I said aloud.

Is it the lies that drive us over the edge, or the truth?

When I reached 59th and 5th, a vibrant clot of girls and women in all shapes and sizes lined up behind a fluttering banner that announced a 5K through Central Park. Their red and white bibs read "Women Running Against Reagan." They aimed to thwart his chances for re-election by running through the park toting water bottles in fanny packs.

Before the starter's gun went off, a female spectator yelled at them, "You need to run FOR something, not against!" One of the runners gave her the finger, setting off the others. "Shaddup, granny!" and "Fuck off, fascist!" Outnumbered, she returned the gesture before slinking off.

I watched them toe the line, then take off in a wave of arms and legs to the entrance to the park. The carriage horses, behind their blinkers, remained unmoved by the surge. They appeared deep within themselves, in a place unreachable by the mad human carnival going on around them—the blaring of taxi horns, the sirens, the clanging lunacy that dragged people from the hinterlands to gawk and take pictures. To get robbed, raped, stabbed, clubbed, shoved in front of trains.

Suddenly, I felt myself shrink down, along with the entrance to Central Park—Alice before she went down the rabbit hole—as the joggers, now tiny too, approached it. Then it gaped large enough to swallow them, then engulf the whole block—the city itself—into its maw in one monstrous gulp. My knees buckled and I had to sit on a bench and lower my head. Normally, I hated being touched, as did Khalika, but when a passing Hispanic woman asked if I was "hokay," I had the sudden urge to hug her to me, weep into her soft bosom, go home to the Bronx with her, where she might make me *arroz con pollo* and put me to bed. Instead, I smiled and said I'd be all right. A runner who showed up late and missed the race offered me her water bottle. After ten minutes or so, I felt better and caught a downtown train to the loft.

Why did I feel like I was losing the plot?

I slept for twelve hours, dreamt I rode Mercutio bareback on a trail that seemed from another era, another place. Without urging, he broke into a trot, then a canter. Suddenly we were lifting off, up, up, steadily and silently until we hovered above the trees. I looked down as if from a plane, everything a miniature, a toy train town. Mercutio galloped on effortlessly, faster still, until we broke free of gravity and floated in deep, silent space. I was delirious with a joy so intense that when I awakened, tears streamed down my face, my hands poised above my chest, as if I had been clutching Mercutio's mane. It was Mercutio, and maybe Rhiannon, coming to my rescue, I decided. After that I felt OK.

New York was brutally hot. On the avenues, I felt nuked, cooked from the inside. My sister had evaporated again in the heat, like mist over the distant hills on the trails we walked together in our grass-stained shorts, sweaters tied around our waists, forearms streaked with salt and dirt from rock hunting. We'd create scenarios for how we'd escape, maybe take the train to Texas and cross the border into Mexico with a bag full of Bianca's baubles.

Since high school, maybe before, Khalika's mantra was always that I needed to toughen up, even when I told her I had reached my limit. She insisted that everything would become clear if I'd only stay the course with her. The world—what inhabited it and drove it—men like Dick, women like Bianca—would gnaw at your flesh, she warned, until it hit bone, then through to the marrow. It could smile while doing it. The goal was to blot out all the beauty, to shroud it before it could rescue you, drag you out of the nightmare men had created by, and for, themselves and the women who aligned themselves with them.

To accomplish her vision, I must, like her, present as a gardenia and close like a Venus flytrap, but faster . . . faster.

"Evil blooms slowly," wrote Baudelaire, "like a flower." To me, it was always there, in the form of my stepparents, of Dollar Man, of all that lurks in the crevices, the shadows, the empty lots that were rapidly being paved over.

Under her tutelage, I aced every test, but refused accelerated learning programs to skip grades at school. Khalika said I was far beyond even the most gifted students, and not just academically, but where it really mattered—my instincts, my vision. I had to believe her, even if I didn't entirely feel it yet.

She used to leave me poems in the barn when she took off, short, cryptic phrases, sometimes in foreign languages I'd have to look up. I got more and more interested in art-house films, especially French ones and film noir. I once found poetry cryptic too but, somehow, always understood hers, almost immediately got the message or, as Jung put it, "the meaning beyond meaning." That's not really a mystery, though. We are a split egg, and people who make it their business to study the strange interaction of twins still don't understand our peculiar and eerie connection. I never had a knack for metaphor, yet hers seemed to break through. "The connection," she said once, "ours is on steroids."

Khalika made sure I understood before she split again. I felt that tension, like something was lurking—under my bed, out the filthy window of the subway as it roared through the dripping tunnels with its dead-eyed cargo. Khalika advised me to ignore it and concentrate on making more money.

"There'll be a quiz on Friday," she'd joke before she skipped off again. Then I realized she never said which Friday.

CHAPTER 2

Sometimes, toward the end of one of my shifts, when I was really bored and beat, I'd face the gold-flecked mirrors that lined the walls behind the platform that extended the length of the bar. I would whisper to myself as I snaked back and forth above the customers, the die hards who didn't vacate until last call. *Eat my asshole*, I'd think, smiling. Or, *Drive off a cliff mid-BJ*.

Once, I thought I caught Khalika's reflection out of the corner of my eye, sitting at the end of the bar. I whirled around, but when I looked into the murk, there was nobody there. Another time, through a curtain of smoke, I saw a guy jerking off at a table toward the back. His cock was huge, like a joke rubber dildo, and he was stroking it lazily, like he had all the time in the world to finish, zip up, emerge from the shadows and order another drink. He smiled up at me and waved, as if he were acknowledging somebody he knew in a restaurant. I turned away, in shock. When I spun around again, nobody was there.

That morning, after that endless shift, waiting on the platform for the meat train, I felt a presence, even though I hadn't heard anyone approaching. When I turned around, a beautiful Black man in an emerald-green shirt stood there, gazing at my back. I felt a chill go through me, even though I felt no sense of danger. I couldn't help jumping though.

"Sorry, you startled me."

"No worries, my baby, my orphan child."

I froze. His voice was like warm silk mixed with a handful of sand. I thought of Marvin Gaye. He even looked a little like him.

"Something big is coming. I can't stay long. Stay awake, my child. Always remember your father. Never forget your mother. They hold the map to that place that may only be circled and never penetrated. The horse knows more than we do. All spirit animals know what we cannot. I love you. Try to stay on the Earth."

I couldn't speak, felt the blood drain from my face.

Then I heard the rumble of the downtown train. Before I could form any words, the man reached out and stroked my hair wistfully, tenderly. Then he looked frightened, spun like a dancer and sprinted down the platform. I almost fainted, managed to get myself together by the time the train screeched to a halt and the doors jerked open. My heart was pounding so hard I was sure all the midnight gamblers could hear it.

I hardly had time to think about what had just happened, because when I got back to the loft, I knew immediately that my twin had visited again. She left an empty champagne bottle, a glass smudged with lipstick, and red pistachio shells all over the counter. She had kissed the bathroom mirror and drawn a face around it.

She has never been neat, only thorough.

She used the key I left for her on the ledge above the door. I went out to the entrance and reached up. There it was.

I could smell her again—so sweet, like a rainy day before the air solidified, became something barely breathable. I don't know what she's up to, why she won't come when I am here. Not yet anyway. I cleaned up after Khalika, made myself a snack, and popped a beer. When I turned away from the kitchen, there, leaning against the wall on one side of the window, was a gift. Did I mention that she paints too? Just like JeanLuc—dark, brooding landscapes with shadowy figures that lurk behind trees, in alleys. I thought of JeanLuc's rendering of Bianca—the death's head bride. This one, too, was done in somber, muddy colors. The dry husk of some plant, the leaves like those of an artichoke, burnt, still trying to reach up to a blighted sun. I walked, reached out and ran my fingers over the image, along a line of ocher she deliberately dripped down around the bottom, outside of where a frame would have been. She left her brushes and tubes, unwashed, on a brown paper bag. It was so Khalika that I laughed.

I do the work; you can do the cleanup.

"Oh Khali," I said out loud to her painted prophecy, "I need you now more than ever. Please don't abandon me. I'm stronger, but I still don't know what I am without you. I would forgive you anything. Please don't go to Mexico without me. Don't go anywhere without me. Please, Khali . . . without you I don't know if I even want to be."

And with that thought, I was flung backward—to half a lifetime ago, when we really did go to Mexico. Dick and Bianca took us on vacation to Puerto Vallarta when we were ten, before they really started to hate each other. I guess they were afraid to leave us with anybody who might sniff out what they were up to.

We walked up a steep trail to the edge of a rock outcropping that extended over the azure water below. Dick and Bianca, sunstruck and drunk, had fallen asleep by the pool in their lounge chairs. We put our shorts on over our bathing suits and slipped away in our flip-flops, leaving them to burn to a crisp.

We made it to the top and as I gazed out at the expanse of blue, Khalika slipped behind me, hugged me before shoving me over the edge. My sustained scream echoed off the rock parentheses of the cliff as I plummeted about forty feet, feet first, into the choppy water. As soon as I made it to the surface, Khalika screamed and plunged in herself, windmilling her arms and bicycling her legs until, at the last possible moment, she twisted her body in the air, executing a perfect jackknife a couple of yards in front of me. I paddled furiously in place, sputtering and calling her a bitch after she surfaced. "We're mermaids," she shrieked, "tails in the water, legs on land. And don't forget it!" *Forget it . . . forget it . . . forget it,* said the echo, as it tailed off in the breeze.

Can we, Khalika? Be anything we want? Or is it just you?

We swam to shore, climbed up and did it again, hand in hand. Khalika screamed, *"Acta non verba!"* into the granite cliff that met the sea in its unbroken, violent tryst. When we got back to the hotel, Dick and Bianca were still frying in the Mexican sun. They had to stay in their room for most of the rest of the week while we explored every day until dark. They pretended to be pissed about it, made threats, smeared on more balm.

The memory made me happy, the feeling of being free of the two monsters as vivid as the reality of those sun-drenched days. We imagined never returning to the hotel, of sprouting tails below our waists and heading out beyond the horizon.

Something made me take another look at Khalika's painting. After I focused on it for a few minutes, I saw it. It swam up into my vision like one of those hidden figures you're meant to finally focus on within a photograph or a drawing. It was a beautiful, slender Black man concealed in the blighted foliage. He wore a green shirt. He was smiling, wistfully, ruefully.

"What's happening here Khalika . . ." I whispered.

I stripped off my clothes.

There was a knock at the door.

CHAPTER 3

I nearly jumped out of my skin, because 1) nobody ever visited me here, and 2) it was 2:00 a.m. I walked to the door in my panties, grabbing the shotgun I keep by the door, racked it and looked out the peephole. It was a man, but not the one from the subway platform.

"Whoever you are, you better have a damned good reason to be here."

My visitor held up a badge. "Lieutenant Mark Vincente, Manhattan Vice," he informed me with his cop delivery. His eyes were the color of the sea around Bermuda. Except where the pink sand would have been, there was caramel.

"You can't come in now. What do you want? I'll meet you tomorrow at the coffee shop downstairs. I'm not dressed for company."

I put the shotgun back.

He laughed, a nice, easy laugh, said he realized that it had been a while since the first interview, but wondered if I remembered DB telling me that they might need to interview me about my stepparents' murder.

"I wanted to call first, but Detective Bruno said you don't have a phone. And I tried to come a couple of times earlier, but you weren't here. Sorry about the hour. Did somebody follow you?"

"I keep irregular hours, and nobody followed me, just something weird happened. Never mind, I can't explain." I was beat, I realized, needed a drink and sleep.

Green Eyes said he was looking into some homicides that might be connected to some unsavory doings and that his investigations so far seemed to point to Naked Envy as one of the origins of this malfeasance.

"Wow, that sounds like some heavy shit. I bet you don't get much of that going on in these places, huh? Hard to tell if it's party in the front, business in the back, or vice-versa, is it?"

"Uh-huh," he said, not missing a beat, "they need to put some kind of warning up at the entrance, like 'Vice is Us.'"

This time, I laughed.

"I wonder if these guys ever open actual laundromats to sanitize the loot."

He laughed again.

"Detective Bruno was kind of surprised to find out you're working in that place. You must need money really bad."

"Girl gotta do what she gotta do. It only bothers me when I see the place with the lights turned on. And you're right: I'm not doing this for shits and giggles."

I'd dropped a bundle on rent and security—made major withdrawals from the cash stash, with Khalika's full approval. The last affordable loft in Soho, apparently. I'm cleaning up in that gilded shithole, so I figured I'd do it as long as I could stand it.

"Uh-huh," he said, putting his face closer to the peephole. His eyes were the brightest green I had seen on a human. They were like Nimrod's.

"I apologize for barging in on you like this, but your late stepfather was chin deep in some major sewage I've been wading around in. I thought I'd fill you in on a few things too, things you might be able to further clarify. I mean, I can share some things that aren't already out there. Your former stepfather was part owner of the bar you're dancing in, but it's not against the law, as long as you're over eighteen."

This wasn't news to me.

"I'm assuming they have no idea who you are?"

"Nope—no clue—and I like it that way. My sister got

me the job. She's a better talker than I am, I mean, when she decides she needs to talk."

"OK, I'll meet you tomorrow, say around noon at that coffee shop. I mean if you're free?" He started to say something, went silent, then realized what I'd just said. "Wait, you have a sister?"

"Yep, a twin. I'll tell you about her tomorrow."

The words came out before I could stop them. I clapped my hand over my mouth. Well, we were free agents now—I guess I didn't need to keep hiding the existence of my vagrant twin from the authorities anyway.

He agreed, said goodnight.

"Hey, you gonna report me to the IRS?"

He smiled and nodded his head yes before he disappeared from the peephole and walked away.

Good sense of humor so far.

I popped another beer, took a bath, and fell into bed. I thought about those eyes, that voice. It took a while to get to sleep. I didn't dream at all—at least not that I remember. When I thought back on that first meeting, through the peephole, I realized I was giddy, and didn't even know why. Something made a decision for me, but it wasn't my head.

CHAPTER 4

I woke up in time to get fixed up for my meeting with Lieutenant Mark. I was intrigued and ready to find out what he knew. I can tell immediately if somebody is just average smart or very—not just by the way they talk, but by their sense of humor. Dumb fucks don't have one, and there's no cure for it. Take the late Dick and Bianca, for instance. They only laughed at the misfortunes of others.

I got there ten minutes early and ordered a coffee. I was nervous. Mark was right on time. I watched him walk in. Over six feet, slender but wiry, like a middle-weight boxer. He walked over to the table with a panther's gait. Although he was dressed casually, he telegraphed elegance. His skin, in the harsh white light, was mocha, his startling eyes almost chartreuse. Nice mix. There's a dancer at Envy who looks like she could be his sister. Mocha Sundae. Khalika and I have green eyes, but they're a different shade, more of a forest at dusk.

He scanned the shop, which was busy, walked over and slid into the booth across from me. He reached across to shake my hand. His was warm, even though it was a frigid February day, cold and windy and not wanting to give up its death grip on the city. Mark ordered a coffee and I took a refill. When the waitress asked if we wanted anything else, he looked at me. The woman seemed to be checking him out and liking what she saw. I told her we'd decide later.

I told Mark that the owners and the guys who run the Envy had no idea who I was, mainly because I looked nothing like the departed. Mark looked at me a beat longer than necessary before he spoke. After a little small talk, Mark got right down to it—told me that it seemed like Dick's associates didn't do what Khalika called "splatters." He didn't put it that way though. He called it "overkill."

"We pulled in a few lowlifes we knew were involved in your stepfather's various business interests, at least the ones who have addresses, and they said no way did they have anything to do with it. Your guardian was worth more alive than dead. I mean, he was still making payments—it's just that they were getting later, and the interest was building up. They wouldn't have killed him unless he just stopped paying. Or at least they would have roughed him up first before doing anything like that. This looked like it was personal. Whoever it was, he, or they, were very angry."

Mark rubbed his chiseled jaw with his thumb. "Detective Bruno thought it might have been one or another of their lovers. It took a lot of work, a lot of rage, to stage that scene."

"I see."

"If anything, it would have been an in-and-out type of hit. They probably wouldn't have killed your stepmother unless they were forced to or unless she was part of the operation. And even then, it wouldn't have been the bloodbath we had here, the . . . posing."

I winced on cue, said nothing.

"Sometimes these guys will want to send a message, but I don't think this was one of those times. A card was left too, like a homemade greeting card, birds and flowers on the front, short message inside. That's not what these types do either."

"So, what are you thinking?"

"Nothing was stolen, nobody got raped, not technically anyway, and there was no evidence of any kind—no prints, hand or foot, aside from family members and the maid. Your guardians didn't have many visitors, did they."

"They were what you might call private. All their socializing, if you want to call it that, was done elsewhere."

Mark added that the alarms were in working order but that they had been disabled from inside. The cameras too.

It was so weird, sitting over coffee with a man I couldn't stop staring at like an idiot. I had never done that before—get all googly-eyed over any boy, man, girl, woman, or anything in between, except maybe one or two on a movie screen. His eyes, yellow and green at once. The sensuous mouth that contradicted the words it formed, the darkness they signified. He told me his mom was Irish and that she still worked checking out groceries, that he was an only child whose dad was killed in Vietnam. He'd gotten a partial scholarship and worked to pay whatever that didn't cover. He'd boxed as an amateur, moonlighted as a bouncer. He'd graduated college with a minor in English lit, then straight into the police academy.

Ever since I knew what sex was, if I thought about it for more than a couple of seconds, I would get sick in the pit of my stomach. Now, coming up on twenty, I felt like a twelve-year-old with her first crush on a movie star. Nothing creepy leaked out of this guy, not from his eyes, his mouth, the tips of his fingers. His charm was real, not faked, like Dick's. He said he was twenty-eight, and I could just tell that he would never think of coming on to anybody he thought of as a kid, especially one he was interviewing, even if that kid did work in a perv bar, basically naked. But this guy—there was some kind of deep sadness that lurked under the cop mask. His eyes, the way they hardened, then softened. I thought of the myth—the guy, doomed to carry that big rock up the mountain, only to have to do it all over again, every day, forever. Khalika would have said he just looked like a hot cop to her, to be avoided at all costs. I would have told her she was getting jaded.

"So, this twin of yours—she obviously hit the bricks a while ago?"

"Yep, she just couldn't handle that particular scene. So she split at intermission. She checks in though, just not often."

Mark stared at me until I felt my ears get hot and my palms started sweating.

CHAPTER 5

We sat there for about an hour, the waitress refilling our coffees until I started to get jittery, strung out. I soon found out what the sadness I'd detected was about. He told me he'd been married and that his wife, after they'd separated, had taken a dive off her condo terrace. She'd been on a cocktail of anti-depressants.

"Because you got separated?"

"Not exactly."

He seemed to be trying to make a decision about whether to tell me.

Then he laid it on me, staring down into his coffee. They had married right after they finished college, where they met, and she'd gotten pregnant almost immediately, even though they hadn't planned it. They separated a couple of years later, after their daughter had been snatched right off a swing in a neighborhood playground while his wife was being kept busy talking to the vampire's accomplice, another "mother" who vanished like smoke immediately after his wife started looking frantically for their baby.

Mark glanced up from his coffee, his jaw muscles twitching.

"Oh God, no," was all I could manage. I thought of Dollar Man, and what Khalika said after I told her about him. "They're everywhere, like filth flies. You get where you can smell them."

"Yeah, no gods around that day, I guess. Nobody minding the store."

Of course, like everybody this has ever happened to, he

101

said, she never forgave herself, even if Mark managed to carry on. He had to, he said, or go mad.

"She got on the anti-depressants in desperation, couldn't function at all. She slept most of the time, hardly ate. Her dosage was upped several times, until she started to hallucinate, walk in her sleep. Maybe that's how she managed to jump. We kept in touch, of course—loved each other—but it became impossible to live together with the grief, the guilt. There's no place to put it, except on each other. It's like drowning."

I could see he was kind of uncomfortable telling me about it, but I think he must have felt an instant kinship with me, two survivors of a plane crash hanging on to the same floating debris. You don't want to revisit the scene again, day after day, year after year, but somehow debris keeps floating to the surface—even in dreams—demanding to be examined before it's pushed down again.

Although things could never be the same, after a certain time, maybe they could just be different and, like a lot of men, he threw himself into the work. He would never give up, he said, looking for his daughter, finding who took her. He'd already called in every marker, picked the brains of anybody who might be able to point him in the right direction. He would never be able to let it go, he said—not until the day he died.

Clenching and unclenching his long fingers, popping his knuckles, he told me of recurring nightmares. He'd see his baby in a stroller, from a distance. Somehow, he would know her by the curve of her cheek, her tiny perfect hands holding on to the bar in front. Before he could get to her, his feet would get stuck in something gluey, deeper until it engulfed him, then the entire street. In another, he had to watch her, as he was held down by a crowd, being tossed into a car, like a rag doll, before it sped away, her face and hands appearing in the rear window, screaming, her mouth a black O, as strangers kept him pinned to the sidewalk. Sometimes the car was a van. Other times, there was no vehicle at all. He'd just look down and she would be gone. Somebody tried to comfort him by saying, in absurd dream logic, "Don't worry, she's all grown up now, she'll be back when she's ready;" in another, "Why don't you check the closets?"

"Her name is Sofia," he said, as if she were still somewhere alive, if he could only figure out where and how to get to her.

It was hard to take in from a man who looked so young, who was, in fact, so young. But it was all there in his eyes, his posture, his low voice that he couldn't quite keep from cracking. Then I thought of what they found in Dick's safes—in the house and at the agency. I didn't know what was happening upstairs at Naked Envy until Khalika filled me in. The crew Dick owed the money to weren't even aware of it. Mark said it looked like a national, possibly worldwide kiddie porn film operation—including sex slavery and even snuff—was being run out of both the modeling agency and Naked Envy. Mark said he was beginning to think the hit was ordered from one of the heads of this hydra, certainly not the goons Dick was making payments to.

Except for sharing his awful story, Mark was otherwise all business that first day.

He asked me to tell him every single detail I could remember about the night of the murders. He was unclear about why I would not have told his colleague about my sister. DB's theory about Dick possibly being involved in the filthy foursome's orgy tapes wasn't shared by Mark.

"He wouldn't have risked it. Not on moral grounds, but because his associates wouldn't have been pleased. These slimy bastards run a tight ship when it comes to talent. It's all about control. No freelancing."

I told him Khalika was around so infrequently, that she was so young when she split, I didn't think it was important, didn't even want to involve her in the whole ugly mess, that she had enough trouble surviving out there, even if she was smart.

"It's an old habit," I admitted. When Khalika ran away for real, we agreed I wouldn't mention her to anyone, especially not the authorities. I told Mark that before we went to the barn, Dick was having one of his routine eruptions at the dinner table and demanded that we "get the fuck out of his sight," and we'd happily complied. Khalika hung out for maybe fifteen or twenty minutes. Then she split. Mark stared at me, enough seconds ticking by to make me start tapping my fingernails on the table.

"I don't know, Violet; I'm trying to put a puzzle together where the pieces have been scattered like gory confetti. I'd like to get in touch with Khalika. I have a feeling she knows more than you do, and that maybe you don't even know how much you know. I don't know how you both came out of your upbringing without more consequences."

"Well, Khalika definitely got herself in plenty of jams, but she's so street-smart, she always found a way out of them. I mean, she's way smarter than I am."

"Do you have any idea where she is now?"

"Nope, and I won't until she's ready to resurface. You won't find her. She's the black cat that merges with the night. You know, like Rhiannon in the song."

I felt that warning twitch at the base of my spine, around my tail bone. *You shouldn't have told him about me*, it said, as if Khalika were sitting beside me, hissing in my ear.

CHAPTER 6

A few weeks later, Mark and I met again at the same coffee shop. I told him that on the night of the slaughter, Khalika made one of her infrequent materializations that, for obvious reasons, made the bastard squirm. Bianca too, since she knew what was going on with Dick—maybe not all of it, but a lot. She knew he'd tried to make a move on me, not that she tried to talk to me about it or intervene. Bianca would never have done that. She would only worry that I or, more likely, Khalika, would snap, maybe report them to the authorities, you know, the same geniuses that put you back in the same place all the shit went down, if they promise never to do it again.

"I told you it was time to split long ago," Khalika had reminded me that final night in the barn, before the last supper, shaking her head and flicking loose hay around with the toe of her boot.

"It's Merc that keeps you tied to this place."

But there was more: I felt the presence of JeanLuc and Oceane sometimes—so strongly that it made me shiver. I felt like one or both would just walk across the pasture and through the barn doors, waving.

You never thought we'd really leave you both with them, did you?

That night: I'll always remember how she slouched, drilling craters in Dick and Bianca with her eyes, not eating, not talking. Lupe didn't even look at her, just kept bringing out dishes, returning with more—always more. Whenever I got the courage to peek over at Khalika, her face was as dark as the sky before the twister forms, undulating in the distance.

Her lank, glossy hair hung in panels, the color of Brazilian rosewood. Her looks always startled me, even though we're identical. She was like the mannequin in the movie that suddenly comes to life and runs amok, while I stay frozen in the pose the window trimmers put me in, waiting for her to kick me in the ass.

"It was like she knew what was coming," I murmured, almost to myself. Mark just looked at me like he was studying a photograph of a crime scene. His eyes clouded up then, and he said he needed to get going. I didn't want him to go, and yet I did. He said he wished I'd get a phone.

When we exited the coffee shop that second time, we walked off in opposite directions, me to the loft, Mark to wherever he had parked.

Before I reached the entrance to the loft, I came upon two women, both dressed in business attire, both shoeless. They were crouched down in front of a shop. When I got closer, I saw that each had her fingers entwined in the other's hair, had two fistfuls of it. They were like two apex predators locked in some kind of silent death dance, where only one would emerge—battered, but victorious, the other succumbing to her wounds or limping off into the distance. They grunted and sweated, as if trying to drag some heavy object, both refusing to release the other's hair. A small crowd began to gather, and I joined them, transfixed. It was like street theatre.

Finally, one of the women let out a high, sustained keening noise—*aiiiiiiieeeeeee, aiiiiieeeeeee*—as her torsade came off in the other's fists, clip attached. She looked at it with surprise before tossing it into the gutter and grabbing hold of the skimpy, exposed hair that had been hidden under it. I stood rooted to the spot. Nobody seemed to want to do anything to separate them; they were enjoying the free show. I turned and walked away, not wanting to see which animal prevailed, which would live to hunt again on the concrete Serengeti.

"One probably banging the other's husband," one male

onlooker murmured philosophically before taking a bite of his bagel, then sipping his coffee.

When I got home, I went straight to the fridge and grabbed a beer, sucking it down in three goes, and lit a cancer stick. What would my liver and lungs look like on an x-ray in twenty years if I stayed in this city, in this lifestyle? How do you wind up like these women, grappling in the street over some worthless dick? Or worse—panhandling, sleeping in a box under newspapers?

I shouldn't feel this spent at twenty.

This gig was definitely getting to me.

I thought of that Eagles song, the one where nobody wants to tell you how far up Shit's Creek we are, how nobody really wants to know anyway.

CHAPTER 7

Lieutenant Mark Vincente
Detective Notes
February 16, 1985

Interview is result of information received from Westchester Homicide. Violet DeLoache is 19 years old and is/was the ward of Dick and Bianca Danzinger, who were killed in their home, a Westchester estate, previously owned by Violet's parents. The murders took place about five months ago, but it's taken until now for the info to permeate from Westchester to NY City Vice, then down to me, and to locate Violet.

Violet's parents were JeanLuc and Oceane DeLoache. Oceane died not long after giving birth to Violet and her twin sister Khalika.

Shortly after their mother died, Bianca moved in as nanny to Violet and Khalika and two years after that, she married the grieving widower. 3 years on JeanLuc DeLoache died in circumstances that have never been totally explained. Bianca inherited everything—other than trust funds that the girls receive at age 21—and became legal guardian to Violet and Khalika.

After that Bianca married Dick Danzinger, whom she had known in school. Up until Bianca marrying JeanLuc DeLoache and inheriting the Westchester place, Dick and Bianca had been longtime petty grifters, small time stuff—check-kiting, some pimping by Dick, Bianca fleecing gullible older guys.

After inheriting JeanLuc's estate, they moved up several leagues. Dick bought into a couple businesses in the city—the reason Westchester passed this on to us. One's a model agency that does a little legit business but seems to principally have existed to get young hopefuls to take part in porn films on the promise of it leading to 'something bigger.' The other is a club on 53rd and Lexington called the Naked Envy. In addition to the usual watered-down liquor, prostitution, and money-laundering, it is believed to be a distribution point for video tapes, not just run-of-the-mill porn, but also underage stuff, and snuff tapes from Mexico.

According to a note from Lt. Loretta Bruno, up in Westchester, Violet was sleeping in a loft in the barn where she kept her horse the night of the murder. The barn's about 100 yards from the house and she didn't hear anything.

The Westchester estate is now sold and any assets the Danzingers had have gone to pay debts. Violet is now in the city, living at 997 Canal Street, Soho, and dancing in the Naked Envy (the management don't know anything about her rela tionship to Dick) as a quick way make enough to support her self and pay for her horse to be boarded until she inherits her trust fund, and maybe goes on to college.

Violet says she was broadly aware of the nature of Dick's business—he never made any effort to hide it at home—but coming up in that atmosphere since she was seven it became background noise to her. She was on bad terms with both guardians—believes they were responsible for the death of her father—and stayed there for her horse, and would have got out in a few years when her trust fund came through.

Violet thinks the murders were hits due to late payments to loan sharks, as he was starting to take some heat on that. It's not typical for loan sharks to kill someone with the potential to keep paying, even if they're late, and Dick was still earning from the club and its various activities. The murder was done in a highly stylized way, and a card with a note in Latin was found at the scene—"Ego pingere in morte tua colores" translated as "I paint you in death with your own colors."

Violet didn't have much other information about the murders, about Danzinger's operation, or anyone who was putting pressure on him other than the loan sharks, or activities at the Naked Envy. Some business seems to be done in an upstairs office there. We left it that she would keep her eyes and ears open while she was working at the Envy and we would keep in touch.

CHAPTER 8

I felt the steady stare of non-male eyes at my back. And yes, I can tell. When I turned around, there she was, looking up at me with that ironic, crooked half smile, the tiny diamond eyes in her *memento mori* skull pendant flashing in the dimness. She wore the blond cornrow wig. I was almost at the end of my shift, and all I wanted to do was climb down, throw on my clothes, and run out with her. I was getting so used to dancing virtually naked that I nearly forgot about it. I mostly liked the girls, their don't-give-a-fuck attitudes, their toughness mixed with the vulnerability of being exposed in front of fully clothed males. There's a solidarity among them that nobody on the outside would imagine. Most customers likely viewed us as interchangeable units; one goes up for twenty minutes, climbs down, and a replacement component is issued from a storage area in the back.

I did this thing on a rope vine bolted into the ceiling that was very popular. I would maneuver my body upside down, work my way around it like a snake. I never crossed a line—never catered to freak tastes. Even if you don't, they imagine scenarios of what they'd do if they had you at their mercy, which for an unknown segment of the male population could include, but not be limited to, forcing you to watch them jerk off, pissing on you, putting cigarettes out on your chest, or slicing you to ribbons.

I'm getting more like Khalika every day, and it's about time. Take me or leave me; it's all the same to me. I think of them the same way they think of me—interchangeable and disposable—no replacement wanted or needed.

I was expecting her to appear, so I wasn't surprised seeing

her perched on a barstool, martini in hand. All my resent-ment drained away; I was just relieved she'd finally decided to check in. I noticed a gauntness that hadn't been there the last time I saw her. Khalika always appeared to subsist on air, alcohol, and cigarettes.

I was picking up her habits, and quickly.

She ran her long index finger around the rim of her glass, smiling up at me. Her nails were painted a deep, glittery pur-ple. She snaked her head back and forth and tapped the bar with her fingernails, which I knew meant that she approved. I turned, grabbed the backs of my calves, peeked through my legs, and waggled my tongue at her. A blubbery guy with a spray of acne on his face and neck—a double-bacon cheese-burger in a yellow polyester shirt—decided it was for him and passed up a twenty. I shoved it in my G-string, smiled and checked the clock: 1:58 a.m.

Khalika downed her drink and slapped a tip on the bar. She jerked her thumb toward the exit, held up five fingers, and split. I climbed down, got my cash from the manager, threw jeans and a shirt over my costume and stuffed my tips into my rucksack.

By the time I met Khalika out front, it was a little after two. She flicked a cigarette butt into the gutter and blew the smoke through her nostrils in a long plume that the wind carried away.

"Happy hatch day, Sparkles. Let the festivities begin, for the witching hour is long gone. It's been too long since we've spoken—I mean in the quivering flesh."

There was something about Khalika that night, from the very start, but I didn't dare ask her what was up; I mean, be-sides our birthday. She was fully capable of erupting on me when she was in one of her blacker moods. This time I was having a hell of a time reading her mood. Sparks were practi-cally flying from her fingertips, as the song goes.

"Where the hell have you been? It's like you dropped off the face of the Earth!"

Khalika didn't respond.

A few stragglers left the bar behind me. One was a regular—one of the weirder little creeps who, I was told, arrived and got taken home in a black limo. He always called you "Miss" followed by whatever you called yourself. The guy called himself Taffy, and he craved discipline and humiliation. He would ask permission to go to the can. He was some kind of executive with *The Daily News* and the night barmaids said he'd leave huge tips if they were mean enough to him. He was all of five feet, four inches in his elevator shoes.

Khalika rolled her eyes as the chauffeur came around and opened the door for him. He slid in, not acknowledging us, like the street outside the bar was a different world. He glanced briefly at us before his coach pulled away from the curb, his pale eyes popping behind coke-bottle-thick lenses.

Another testosterone giant emerged in a leather motorcycle getup, the jacket covered in studs, "Aliens" lettered across the back. He saluted us, mounted his chopper, and roared off.

"Tasty," said Khalika. "Bet he'd like to show us his clubhouse, do us on the pool table."

She has never been a hugger, so we just stood there grinning for a few seconds before she spun on her heel and headed north on Lexington. Khalika joked that I should get Taffy to come over and clean the loft after she'd dropped in, that while he was at it, he could lick out the bowl, but only if he was a good boy. I laughed and said it was not out of the question, that I could imagine him in his maid uniform.

Then Khalika said, all nonchalant: "Remember when Dick-o said that if you didn't get your act together, he'd sell Mercutio or ship him off to the killers? I remember the look on your poor little face, like you were imagining all the terror your friend would go through before they put the air gun between his eyes. The same look his recruits probably had when they realized what was up. I knew you'd have that shit in your head for the rest of your natural life."

"How could I forget? Nothing the fucker ever said to me compared to that one."

"But look at you now! I mean, anybody who saw us separately wouldn't be able to tell us apart, except for the wig and my macabre jewelry. Even your eyes are starting to look like mine—your windows to the soul." She smiled wolfishly. "You've dropped a little weight too, but it's all good. It looks like you're laying off the potato chips. That's what I've always hoped for—that you'd finally see that accommodation and placating doesn't work. Ever. There's always more they want to carve out of whatever's left of you. I told you, you must always do what's necessary, Violet, sometimes more than that."

Khalika fingered the skull and spoon on the black cord, stopped for a moment and faced me. "I've wanted to see you for the longest time, but I've been engaged elsewhere. It takes a lot of planning to arrange these meetings. People are looking for me."

When I asked what people, she just set her jaw and continued burning up the pavement.

"I hope you liked what I left at the loft. You must know I'd never abandon you for too long. So, let's embark on our journey via the lower intestine of this crumbling metropolis, for 'tis the shank of the morning, and we are entering our final year as mere sprouts, tender bait for all the untethered freaks roaming this wasteland of plenty."

I gathered my courage and told Khalika about the incident on the subway platform with the beautiful Black dude, the hidden figure in her painting. She seemed unfazed. Her casual response shocked me.

"Oh, that's just Daddy visiting. It's quite a feat, and the conduit usually freaks out. I knew all about it, even what he said. He's right about something big coming; I'm just not sure what it is myself. I mean, you can feel it in the air. I'm going to share something with you soon, and these visitations are only a small slice of the bigger mystery. Daddy is, or was, only an extension of it, as we are. But for this morning, let's just be two sisters celebrating their birthday. Deal?"

"Deal," I whispered, and the word was taken by the wind.

CHAPTER 9

B ut I couldn't forget it. My mind reeled as we walked. Khalika's rucksack bulged with what I assumed was overnight gear. She read my thoughts and said she didn't intend to stay over—she had things that needed doing. She told me she'd seen me once with Mark and asked if anything was heating up.

"Not that I'm following you or anything."

I told her that, of course, there was nothing, reminded her of my revulsion when it came to sex. She gave me a funny, quizzical look and said that wasn't what she was picking up.

"Would you just quit? You're making me nervous. He's a good guy who's been through some heavy shit."

"OK, just watch yourself."

"He said he was investigating what was going on with Dick's side business—that the overkill didn't look like it was done by the loan sharks. He thinks it's possible it was real monsters of the deep that were responsible."

I waited for her reaction, which didn't happen.

"The guy is damaged, by the way. His family is gone—the daughter snatched, followed by the wife taking a header off the terrace. He's hot to crack this pedo ring, and I gotta admit, I'm really down with that, even if another pops up right in its place."

"Yeah, we're all on the same page. A light-hearted threesome, for sure."

Khalika picked up the pace some more. I almost had to jog to keep up. The wind was whipping, cyclonic on the cross streets. The main avenues were lined with colossal, windowed tombstones. Whatever went on behind the windows, in the streets below them, the keepers of order seemed unable or unwilling to keep up with it, were throwing in the bloody towel. Khalika said that if you believed there was any evil you thought hadn't been done sometime, by somebody, you would be wrong.

We passed a cardboard box with two ratty sneakered feet sticking out, an empty bottle on the pavement next to it. It looked like the guy inside might be dead, frozen solid on a street in one of the richest cities, in what was, for now, one of the richest decades there'd been. "Fraud is the sister of greed," somebody said. Even in that cold, the stench was almost overwhelming. The guy was decomposing in his box. Khalika made no comment, forged ahead. The mood seemed to be getting less festive by the minute.

"Dick was a very busy boy," she finally said. "He didn't sit around with his thumb up his ass. I suppose that was why they chose a different finger."

She peeked at me, gave a little snort.

"I really hated that grifting fucker and his whore—maybe more than you did. The threat about your pony sealed it for me, that he would take the one thing that kept you attached to the land they stole, a temporary oasis in the midst of what? How do you even put a name to it?"

Khalika's pea coat was wide open and flapping, and she didn't seem to care. I shoved my hands down in my jacket pockets, lowered my head. The March wind howled like a lost banshee down the canyons of some remote planet, kicking up grit and molecules of frozen shit—dog and human. I pulled my hood up. We passed another of the town's semi-living refuse, this one curled up under some stairs, wrapped in flapping newspapers, a beanie pulled over his eyes.

Maybe freezing to death isn't the worst way to go—like drowning.

At least past a certain point.

Happy fucking birthday.

Something big is coming, my orphan child . . .
Stay awake . . .
Was he going to let me know how far it's gone, maybe past
the point of no return? Are we supposed to join you and Oceane?

CHAPTER 10

Cue up the intro to "Gimme Shelter" by the Stones, which will continue, sporadically, in the background throughout Khalika's version of a girls' night out.

We descended into the gullet of the subway a few blocks from the Envy—down, down into the claustrophobic, airless tunnels to the dripping platforms that, in these hours, were the stuff of horror movies. The screaming, gyrating train lurching to a stop, a pause in its grim, repetitive mission—loading and disgorging the lost, the disenfranchised, the pregnant, the doomed revenants. One or two unlucky voyagers might never make it—devoured by whatever lurked in the alleys, the dripping tunnels, the exclusive clubs of a city deemed by visitors as "a great city to visit, but you wouldn't wanna live there."

Not unless you have more loot than an Egyptian pharaoh, that is. Then you could look down from your penthouse at the abject devastation and sip your cocktail, secure in the knowledge that it could never invade your lavishly appointed, armed camp, fuck up your shit beyond all recognition and be gone before you drain out on the Italian marble floor, the perfectly faded antique Aubusson carpet. Ask Dick and Bianca. Ask any of them. Safe havens exist only in the imaginations of those without any.

We dropped our tokens in the slot, following along behind a few other hunched, subterranean sleepwalkers, graveyard shifters, feeders on the unwary, the dozing. A few unhinged spelunkers seem to have started a mini-craze—shoving oblivious, would-be passengers to the tracks below. I thought of *Dawn of the Dead*, a perennial favorite, and *Return of the Living Dead*.

But with my sister, there was no fear—ever.

My twin spoke. "Wake up and grab your crotch or something—you look like a victim. The meat wagon is coming."

I was a little anxious about being included in her magic orbit again after so many weeks, but I was traveling, by subway in the wee hours, with my badass sister. I couldn't stop smiling.

"Emily's filthier coach approaches, minus any civil fellow travelers. Maybe a couple weenie wagers for giggles?" She made a fist around an imaginary dick, moved it up and down, grinning. A shivering dude on the platform spat into the rails and gave her a sneering sidelong look. That made her repeat her performance until the guy moved away.

Khalika shrugged. "Dunno what his problem is."

We laughed at some graffiti on the white-tiled walls—a smiling giant hard on with balls done in magic marker, a cryptic scrawl: "Filthy cooking bastards" and a straightforward "Jennifer sucks cocks in hell with her mom."

"Well, I have a cunning stunt in mind tonight, my little equine goddess. Just watch. What do you want to bet that as soon as we get on that rolling fart box, choices will need to be made?"

"Isn't that always the way it is?"

"Pretty much."

The platform was quiet as an isolation tank, except for the steady drip of dirty water plinking on the tracks from the street above, echoing off the cruddy walls, and puddling in the spaces between the rails. Our coach roared and clattered in, came to a wheezing stop. We got on and Khalika motioned to sit down across from a girl who looked both bored and nervous. She wore a green army jacket with a sweatshirt under it with the hood pulled up, shadowing her face.

Talk about a victim. This girl was practically flashing a

neon sign. Khalika spread her legs wide enough to nudge the nasty looking druggie she'd deliberately sat next to, whose own thighs were also spread to the max. He had a face like congealed oatmeal with a couple of raspberries tossed in. She made eye contact with him; he looked away. They hate that— the eye contact—makes them think you're packing something they don't want to deal with. Like maybe you're a plain-clothes cop or an off-duty one. I saw that the guy had already mentally crossed us off his list of ladies to mess with, and he fixed his eyes on the poor little green riding hood across the aisle, who averted her eyes, like almost every woman would.

But not my sister. Not me. Not anymore.

CHAPTER 11

Khalika, all casual, reached inside her jacket, extracted a switchblade, flicked it open, and began to whistle through her teeth. She pulled a bandana from her pocket and began to polish the blade—an up and down motion; slowly, steadily—until the ugly, chalky bastard next to her got uncomfortable and moved several feet away. He wasn't worried enough to take his skanky ass to another car, but appeared to be getting angry, frustrated. He kept his focus on the girl, occasionally glancing at Khalika and me. Whenever the girl looked up, there he was, scoping her with his speed-crazed orbs. "Just your type, huh," Khalika called out to the girl, jabbing her thumb at the guy. The girl said nothing, lowered her head, almost smiled.

"Fuck you, dyke," said the prince, to which Khalika responded, amiably, "Not even if they fumigated your ass and transplanted a pair of balls between those twig legs."

I almost knew what she'd say before she said it, and I started to laugh. The girl just looked down again. That shut him up though. One look at her and most skels know not to escalate things. Khalika continued her polishing, like it was the best activity in the world. She held the blade at arm's length and admired it. Finally satisfied, she flicked it closed and put it away.

A tall, chill Black guy eyed the scene with just the slightest show of amusement visible mostly around his eyes, which connected with Khalika's. She winked at him. Some poor bastard, way down at the end of the car, was scrubbing his face, over and over, with a sheet of paper towel he pulled off a roll under his arm. He'd throw the used sheet on the floor, tear off another, and repeat the excruciating ritual. His face was like mashed strawberries, and still he scrubbed, trying to eradicate a stain somewhere in the coils of his brain. Another guy across from him, a Bernie Goetz type, watched everything going on, paranoid, ready to bolt at any sign of confrontation. He got off at the next stop.

A lurching drunk migrated from another car, stinking like a dead man dumped in the desert. He continued on, slurring the words to a song about not getting what you want, but maybe what you need, his breath wafting out like rotten meat in a pan you forgot about for a week.

"You said it, dude," commented Khalika, but the guy just kept massacring the tune until he pulled a bottle from his pocket, laughed, took a swig, and disappeared into the next car. Another guy ground his teeth, describing to himself and us what he was going to do to some bitch who made off with his stash, if he could just find her.

Considering the hour, this cattle car was really jumping. Was it a full moon or something? I'd forgotten to check. When the train stopped at the next station, a sleeper suddenly bolted awake, looked at the sign, and muttered, "Fuck," when he realized he'd missed his stop. He jumped up and flung himself through the closing doors. As soon as one traveler vacated, another took his place.

Besides the girl across from us, Khalika and I were the lone females.

That girl might not have looked like a pushover to anybody but a connoisseur. But what is my sister if not a specialist of the lawless, dead hours, of dead ends where even demons fear to ply their trade? She wears no masks. It's all there, on her face. *Like it or go fuck yourself.* I am the one always trying on different faces, or at least I was. I didn't know how else to be—how to keep contained what must be contained. I think sometimes that I have gone mad, in the shadows, although my sister assures me that is not the case. But I ask how can it not finally bubble up, lava erupting from your throat and spewing out in a geyser, covering everybody around you while you watch the skin fall off their bones in the molten ash of a fury you never acknowledged until the moment when no alternative existed?

CHAPTER 12

A few stops later, the girl got up, her eyes darting left and right. Sure enough, our dream man popped up a couple of beats after her.

"So soon," Khalika murmured. "I thought we had something going on here."

He flipped us the finger before exiting.

A few seconds before the door closed completely, Khalika jumped up and jammed her boot between the doors, popping them back open. The hyena didn't even look around, just stalked the girl at a distance.

We exited to the street, the wind whipping, scurrying trash up and down the block. Snow pelted us in wet, heavy flakes. Khalika's jacket remained open. The girl didn't turn around, leaned into the wind. She didn't want to know. There was a crummy diner open, and she slowed her pace, almost decided to go in, changed her mind. She must have had some sense that she was being stalked, I thought, but decided to dismiss it.

Always a bad idea.

She looked around as we passed a clot of loud, posturing teenagers hanging out on a corner, smoking, spitting out a string of machismo bullshit in Spanish, "pendejo" and "maricon." They made the usual sucky noises at the girl, one pronouncing her flaca, laughing. The girl hung a left, her pursuer now within a few yards of her.

So intent was his pursuit, he never thought to look behind him.

As we approached the pack, their feral sense seemed to pick something up in Khalika, and maybe in me too. *Don't do it. Not these two.* Like any street-corner warriors, they didn't want to risk damage, be called out in front of their pack. They hunched over, pulled their collars up, sucked on their fags. *Maybe it's too cold to bother.*

One tried anyway, just for the hell of it. "Hey flacita," said he, "ju wanna party?" Khalika looked at me, as if inviting me to come up with a retort. Without missing a beat, I looked straight at him and said, "Sure, your box or mine, fuckstick." They all hooted as one, but I could tell it was a charade performed by the pack, for the pack.

"Ju got a dirty mouth for such a pretty bitch," another offered as we rounded the corner.

"You've been practicing," Khalika said, a note of admiration in her voice.

After a few more blocks, the wind and snow took a brief break and it went dead quiet. The weak sodium lights flickered, died, popped on again. No light shone in any window in the apartments lining the block. Ordinary mayhem was easily ignored, except perhaps by the sleepless. A siren shrieked feebly somewhere in the distance.

The twitchy stalker started his silent Nike sprint. Khalika kept pace behind, and I did the same. The girl didn't hear him as he closed the distance, came up behind her, locking his forearm around and across her throat. *Don't scream, don't fight.* We saw the flash of the blade he pulled from his sleeve, held to her throat before he maneuvered her into the crevice. The girl had gone limp with terror, a deer slung over the hood of a car.

CHAPTER 13

Pump up the volume on "Gimme Shelter," right before Merry Clayton shrieks out her solo about rape and murder. Now, it's just a few steps away.

"OK, intrepid disciple," Khalika murmured, almost to herself, "it's that time. I think we can both agree, a woman's work is never done."

We pulled up at the entrance to the narrow fissure, and I stood, transfixed, as Khalika lifted her arms and slipped on, like a surgeon, a pair of blue vinyl gloves she'd extracted from her jacket, along with a black cosh. She tapped the instrument on her right palm a couple of times. "Crude, I know," she whispered, "but an OK opener. Wait here, tiny dancer, you don't need to see this yet. I'm goin' in. You'll know when it's over." Then she handed me a flashlight.

"Hold this please. But don't use it unless I tell you."

She cocked her head to one side like a hawk about to descend on a mouse, and curled from the street into the Stygian blackness of the alley, barely illuminated by the barest sliver of a new moon. I heard the faint sound of the girl sobbing, begging him to let her go, that he could have her bag, that she had a kid waiting at home.

I thought then, right in the middle of it, how I always knew somehow that this had been coming, like the faintest rumbling of a distant train, a tornado. I never wanted to confront Khalika, because along with my fear was this almost sexual thrill I got from thinking of what she might be up to out there—those long stretches where she'd come back looking like a sated cat. Now, here it was—no more imagining or vague twinges of dread about what this rogue goddess might be up to. I saw it like a lightning flash before the house goes up in flames.

She'd been painting the town redder than a daimon's eyes.

And now I would be her accomplice, would bear witness.

It didn't seem to matter anymore. I'd never felt better or freer in my entire stunted life, one made possible with blood-soaked money from my stepfather's pursuits, the same money that delivered Mercutio to me, and the paddock in which he galloped and bucked.

Seconds later, I heard a faint, wheezing croak—"What the fuck . . . cunt?"—and then a blunt thud, like a hammer striking a melon, followed by the clang of metal on concrete. He had fallen over a garbage can on his way down, was now splayed out in the cracked, litter-strewn alley with one whack to the back of his head. All the windows lining the alley remained dark.

Almost immediately after he hit the pavement, his proposed meal came barreling straight toward me, nearly running into me, hardly seeing me. Her breath was ragged, her eyes glazed with shock. She had startled a rat, and it scampered across my shoe. The girl's adrenalin sent her sprinting down the street, back the other way, to the relative busyness of 7th Avenue, until she was swallowed by the night. She didn't even scream. Still, there wasn't much time.

You'll be OK now.

I wasn't even aware of the cold anymore. Blood pounded in my ears as I sucked in big gulps of frigid air. There was no way I could stand there a second longer. Against Khalika's advice, I started to make my way into the alley, flashlight in hand.

And then I heard it.

It wasn't a human sound, nor was it that of any animal I'd ever heard. It was like an alien wind, a sustained, unearthly wail containing both ecstasy and grief. It poured out into the dark sky, pierced it like a blade through black silk.

"OWWWWWWOOOOOOOOOooooooooooooo . . . OWOOOOOOOOOOooooo . . ." The howl tailed off at the end like the mourning whistle of a long-departed train to Gehenna. I was rooted there, and I saw that these ungodly sounds were coming from my sister's throat, seemed, suddenly, to be emanating from my own as well, as if in sympathy.

There was Khalika. She was crouched over the inert lump on the ground like a gargoyle on the parapet of some ancient Parisian church. Her jacket gaped open, her head thrown back as if in the throes of orgasm. The cords in her neck were distended and gray-blue. I shone the flashlight on the scene. Her contorted face, in the focused beam of light, was the color of pewter.

She bayed again, and a single light blinked on in one of the windows above. She was the lone she-wolf on a ridge line, in some part of the back country that man hadn't yet invaded, conquered, ravaged.

I caught the glint of her switchblade, watched as she applied it to the lump's bony naked back, glowing calcium-white. The streetlights flickered again but stayed on. The light in the window went dark. She made quick work of whatever she was doing to his back before she peered up at me, undisturbed by my arrival.

"I think he shat himself," she informed me cheerfully. "I can smell it. Flashlight off, please."

This was it—that instant when everything changed again—like what happened after the invasion. Back to Dollar Man, those four enterprising classmates. Time froze, then picked up again, drawn out and unreal, the dream you can't fully awaken from. If I lived for eons, I would never forget her face in that alley. It contained all the frigid cruelty of all the gods in the pantheon.

Had my nightmares foretold this?

Khalika looked up from her labor, told me she was almost done, that I should keep watch. I could hardly move.

The lump was barely moaning. The wind lifted Khalika's hair, swirling it around her terrifying face. Somewhere on our journey, she had removed the blond wig, but I couldn't say where or when. It was then that I, or something independent of me, conjured Kali—the Goddess—in that narrow defile. I saw the tip of a red tongue emerge slowly from between dark-blue lips and lengthen, until it was level with her skull necklace, then farther, until it almost skimmed her waist.

"Was it good for you?" I heard her inquire, all solicitous concern to the prone, pale lump. She pulled him around to face her, hissed, "Look at me, sweet prince. Look at your final sex partner. I choose this new morning to spare your life. Don't waste it trying to find me. And tell your friends."

Khalika dropped him back on the cracked pavement. He could only moan now, and drool.

"Please . . . stop . . . I'm . . . dead." He wept like an infant.

"Not quite," Khalika said, before rising from her crouch. "Only your dick is. Oh . . . and your arms and legs."

I looked up. All the windows were dark.

"OK. We need to get the fuck out of here."

CHAPTER 14

As soon as I could move, I backed away, almost tripping and falling over some loose trash. I stood guard there until Khalika emerged like a wraith through a black curtain. I was fully complicit now, I understood, and a wave of nausea nearly overwhelmed me. Khalika was cool again, looked exactly as she did when she appeared behind me at the Envy. She smiled, shoved her rucksack, containing the blunt paraphernalia of mayhem, into my trembling hands.

For just a moment I had the eerie feeling that we had merged, were as one now. I imagined I saw a double image reflected in the unfathomable pools behind the transparent lenses of her back-country eyes. I was beyond words, questions—beyond myself—as we walked in silence back to the train. The street was silent and frigid—a moonscape devoid of all life but our own.

"What just happened?" I asked, stupidly.

"Nothing and everything," she replied. "I'm fucking with the natural order of things is all."

We jogged to the train, caught the downtown express, and Khalika got off at the first stop, didn't tell me where she was going or anything else. All I got was, "Be cool, see you when I see you, don't open the door to strange men, and don't leave my tools on the train, birthday girl. I'm serious, shove it back behind the boxes."

Presumably, I was in charge of the evidence.

I held the rucksack to my chest, staring straight ahead. I always carry a blade, and this night was no different. I was suddenly calm. Whatever freaks were on the train would pick that up, like any other night predator. *Move on . . . find an easier one.*

I was exhilarated and nauseated, almost relieved that Khalika had split. I needed some time to process this.

My sister was a killer. I was suddenly certain she had done this before. And so what? Who had she dispatched, I wondered, who didn't have it coming a hundred times over? Just like Dick and Bianca had it coming—that and more. I hoped she would tell me about them. Had I somehow known this all along, tucked away somewhere in the tangle of days? I knew Khalika worked in the deepest, most remote shadows, without distraction, without input from the keepers of order. She had told me so.

"You want to unsee what you have seen and put us both in the cross hairs," Khalika once said through clenched teeth.

I awoke to my environment like a sleepwalker and rummaged through Khalika's rucksack. It contained the gloves, a thin wire, a loaded syringe of something, and a small flashlight. My train was empty except for a homeless woman curled up in a corner seat, arguing with somebody in a dream, taking charge of her situation.

Something is missing. What is it?

My stop. I got off and quickly covered the blocks to the loft, my querencia. I heard the far-off scream of fire engines, the impatient blare of a taxi horn, even at this hour. My watch said 4:20 a.m.

So much had happened in a couple of hours that it seemed, in hindsight, like a scene from a movie, the montage, where time must be compressed to fit the story into it. The lights faltered again, and this time remained off. In a couple of hours it wouldn't matter. At least the electricity waited to crap out until I got off the train. Small mercies.

I pulled out the flashlight, opened the vestibule, and made my way upstairs. The antique elevator was out. I got the loft door open and entered, immediately locking and bolting the reinforced door behind me. I dropped Khalika's equipment, peeled off my winter gear, and hung it on the rack.

After I had settled down, I realized the loft was pretty chilly. I threw on a sweatshirt and went to get a beer. Then I set a couple of logs in the old, sooty fireplace, threw some newspaper on for kindling, and lit it. I went to the bathroom, looked in the mirror and stuck my tongue out—way out—until it touched my chin. I smiled at my image.

Suddenly, I felt fucking great. Better than great—invulnerable almost. It felt like the first time I saw Mercutio, climbed on his back and felt his hydraulic gait. It was as if I had just discovered some occult secret. *This is what it feels like to be alive, what it feels like to find what you've been missing.*

Of course, it couldn't last. What does? Still, it was one hell of a morning.

It hit me then—the switchblade! But when I recounted the events of that surreal scene, I realized Khalika must have wiped it and shoved it back in her jacket. I pulled mine out of my boot and put it back where I always keep it—on my nightstand.

CHAPTER 15

The dreams, or night terrors, started again, with a vengeance. They were more frequent even than after the invasion. They were the sort where you think you're awake, but you're not; you're somewhere in between. I used to get them when I was very young, then again in high school, when I was picked on for being weird, creepy, unsexy, too smart, too naïve, too anything they didn't understand. "Fuck 'em all" was Khalika's attitude.

These vivid dreams, more like visions, usually occurred around dawn. Sometimes, they'd seem to last only a few minutes, with great swaths of disjointed time passing. People communicate like those in a *folie a deux* film or those creepy clowns in Hamlet—where one knows what the other is saying, even if it's all garbled. I'd wake up sweaty or cold, having kicked off or cocooned myself in the bedspread. In one, Khalika was really mad at me, spewing venom—the words made no sense—something about me being stuffed in a sewer pipe, bloated and covered with flies.

"You exist still because of me!" she shrieked, and burst into flames.

In another, I was staring at the wall in my bedroom when suddenly something spoke gibberish into my ear, like an invading entity in a movie. I jerked awake and ran from the bedroom, shaking all over. Some beads hanging from the entrance to the rear area of the loft swayed, clacking as if in a breeze, though no window was open. I went to look, knife in hand, but there was nothing there except the cartons I'd packed from the house. I couldn't get back to sleep, so I got up and made coffee.

In a different one, I tried to move, but something held me down, its breath on my neck, fetid and hot. It finally let me up and when I was able to turn and face the window, I saw a figure—Khalika, yet not her—almost reptilian, kneeling on the fire escape, blood dripping from her mouth and down her chin. She was the age she was around the Dollar Man incident, tall and gangly, her hair in a tangle. She smiled huge with her red clown mouth, then waved and started down the fire escape. I tried to reach her, but I was glued to the mattress, paralyzed. When I was able to move, I got up to check the window. It was open, even though I never leave windows open before I go to bed. I must have sleepwalked.

Even when I was fully awake, I'd walk into the living area or the bedroom and feel sure Khalika would be sitting downstairs in her blond wig, facing the window. She'd be holding a drink in one hand, the other hanging languidly over the back of the couch. She'd be wearing her carnelian scarab ring on her pointer finger, her eighteenth-century *memento mori* skull and jade opium spoon hanging between her breasts on a black silk cord. She jokingly called these items her "statement pieces," ones she'd stolen from a display case on one of her walkabouts.

Something else was starting again too. I sometimes couldn't tell if I had done something in a dream—had a conversation with somebody, an argument—or if it really happened. I found myself asking others if such and such had happened. They had no idea what I was talking about.

I could almost smell Khalika sometimes, as if she'd just gone out the door or down the fire escape. Did I sleepwalk? I didn't know, but once I woke up to go to the bathroom and the mirror was steamed up, the toilet unflushed, the water tinged with red.

Last night, I dreamed we were mermaids, long green hair like seaweed pouring out behind us, our silver tails propelling us through clear, Bermudian waters. Suddenly the sea became as dark and murky as the East River, and naked bodies started floating by, their eyes milky and staring, some with stumps for hands, or headless. We got separated by all the bodies and the water became opaque with blood until all I could see were her silver scales winking farther and farther in the distance. Through the impenetrable crimson soup, I saw that I had lost my tail. I was drowning in the blood, salty as seawater.

I woke up gagging and weeping, almost puking.

I was to have no peace in sleep that morning either, but this dream was different.

Sometime before dawn, I jumped on Mercutio bareback and rode him naked, bent forward over his neck. Something began to chase us, and no matter how fast Mercutio ran, the thing kept up. I pulled Mercutio up and he wheeled, kicked at the amorphous, faceless thing, reared, spun, and ran on. But the pursuer righted itself, continued to run with us until I pulled Mercutio up, dismounted, and faced the thing. It whirled away from us, tried to disappear into the fog-shrouded woods around us. I took off after it on foot, ran it down, tackled it from behind. I brought it down, turned it over and jabbed at its featureless face. With a superhuman strength, I reached deep into where its chest might be and scooped out its heart. It made no sound, only squirmed under me. I held the still beating organ in my palm, tasted it, then held it aloft. A humanoid face swam into view, became more distinct, its mouth becoming a black O of disbelief and horror. Dollar Man. But this time he had no eyes. Just two black holes to go with the toothless, gaping mouth.

I held the pulsing thing, took another bite, and laughed. It tasted sweet—like triumph, or revenge. Like fare fit for the gods. I wiped the gory mess from my mouth with the back of my hand just as Mercutio trotted up. When I lifted my head, Khalika stood there next to my fabulous beast, the necklace of skulls dangling from her hand. In her other hand, she held Mercutio's bridle.

"What is a poet who kills? Why would you ask? *Owooooooooooo . . . owwwwooooo . . . owooooooooooo . . .*" she howled into the mist-shrouded wood surrounding the kill.

I had found out how to enter my own dream and guide it. Could I do it again? Had Khalika, or JeanLuc from beyond the grave, found a way to whisper in my ear?

Own your power. Do it before you are owned. Before you are sucked under. Try to stay on the Earth—above it.

CHAPTER 16

What happened in the alley took on the quality of a dream too. There was nothing in the news about the would-be rapist. Random killings—whatever is short of that—that happen to throwaway people, well, that's just the way it is.

Mark and I met up several more times. Things were heating up in the investigation into the doings at the agency and the Envy. I could tell Mark was wary of getting overly friendly, too personal—for obvious reasons—but I couldn't deny the attraction was there—for both of us. It went beyond shared tragedy and loss into territory totally unfamiliar to me. His eyes told me of places that words would never visit. If he touched my hand, even accidentally, I felt the shock of desiring what had always repulsed me. I was hoping that what didn't happen in the jangle of my waking hours might do so in dreams. I waited. And then it really happened.

One day, over drinks, Mark asked if we might spend a day together—do something fun to blot out, just for a few hours, the ugliness of what had happened, what was still happening, to both of us. Later, he said, we could grab dinner.

The anticipation: it was like the week before Mercutio was delivered, yet there was something else too, a different kind of flutter in my stomach. Whatever it was, I was into it.

We made plans to go out to the north shore of Long Island, where I boarded Mercutio. Becky, the owner of the little farm, had inherited it from her uncle who made it big on Wall Street but never married. He'd died of a stroke five years prior. She said she never wanted to leave the place, even to go shopping. The taxes were paid out of his estate too. She boarded horses because she loved them—loved the lifestyle.

I hadn't seen Mercutio much; being carless, I had to take the LIRR, then get a taxi to the barn. Things had gotten too crazy, too fast. But he was always on my mind. I called Becky weekly to see how he was doing. "Great," she'd say, but she could tell he missed me. He wouldn't put up with anybody else riding him either, so Becky would turn him out in a grassy paddock where he ran, bucked, snorted, and rolled to his heart's content.

On the day Mark and I pulled up at the barn, Merc must have heard or sensed our approach from at least a mile away, because he let out a sustained roar of excitement and stretched his neck out the door of his stall, called again before banging the stall door with his hoof. I ran up to his stall, threw my arms around his neck. I unlatched his door and entered. He was trembling all over, smelling me and rubbing his face up and down my body, nostrils quivering. He made soft little wickers of joy and concern, took the lapel of my jacket in his teeth and pulled me to him. Then he wrapped himself around me. He was beside himself, almost frantic, and I realized I had begun to cry as I inhaled his sweet breath and buried my face in his mane. He seemed to know something had happened, had picked it up from afar—almost like Khalika would. Except this was a different species—one that could read you like a book.

"I've never seen anything like that."

"He does it all the time, but he's really excited today. He's my main squeeze, and he knows it."

"You must miss him, being so far away. You should move him closer to you."

"I'm thinking of moving out here, actually—maybe going to school somewhere. Maybe take up English lit, French, whatever. The strip business is warping my mind—even further. I mean, it's not stripping if you start out almost naked."

I laughed, and so did Mark.

"Anyway, he's pretty happy here, except for missing me. He doesn't have the fifteen-acre paddock he had in Westchester, but as long as he has me, he's OK. Nobody else can handle him. He even dumped me a few times before I found a way to stay glued to his back. He's an off-track thoroughbred, and he cruises at thirty-five miles an hour."

Mark put his closed hand up for Merc's nostrils to sniff. Horses never forget you after that. I gave Mark a piece of carrot to give him, to seal the deal.

"Somebody tried to exercise him once—some guy who thought he was an expert, and he dumped him in a pond. Becky could ride him, but she said it was like riding a whirlwind. She didn't want to take chances these days, since she was pretty busted up—had some pins in her—from some spills she took as an exercise rider at Belmont. Even when Mercutio raced, which he did until he fractured a sesamoid bone at four, he had a female jock. Because he hadn't proven himself in major races, he was slated to be donated to a local horse rescue rather than go to stud. Dick bought him right off the shithead owner, who had, only a month earlier, posed with him in the winner's circle after his first race. Maybe Dick hoped I'd break my neck. The owner was happy to be rid of the expense. Now he can jump too, not that all horses can't."

I took Merc's velvety nose between my thumb and forefinger and gently squeezed it. "Right, Merc? You take a four-foot fence like it's a log." Mercutio's eyes shone with pleasure.

"It must be great to have a way to get outside yourself. I mean, now and then."

"Yeah, for sure. I told my sister that I started out as just a regular girl, but Mercutio made me a goddess the first time I climbed up on him. Anyway, let's see how you take to it—I hope . . . I hope . . ."

Becky appeared from around the other side of the barn.

"It's about time—he's ready to jump out of his gorgeous black skin."

"Sorry it's been a while. Life interfered."

I introduced Becky to Mark.

"I know he's in capable hands. Is he eating OK?"

I rubbed the white exclamation mark on Mercutio's forehead.

"Yep." She smiled brightly. "Except for the past couple of days. He must have sensed your plans and didn't clean his bowl. I'm sure he will later though. I always know you're coming as soon as he does. He starts to pace. It's either that, or he knows you're up to something."

I smiled, knowing what she meant.

Becky offered Mark, who had only ridden a handful of times as a kid, a nice, calm gelding. She tacked the sweet boy up for Mark as I got Merc ready, brushing him to a burnished ebony. "Enjoy," Becky said, before excusing herself to muck out her own mare's stall. Bella Strega was a gorgeous gray Arabian, and Mercutio was in love with her too, calling out to her across the aisle whenever Becky put her away after a ride. Even Nimrod liked Bella Strega, meandering back and forth between her stall and Merc's. Nimrod greeted me effusively too, buzzing like a madman.

We rode for a couple of hours, until Mark complained that he didn't think he'd be able to walk later. I told him it might hurt for a while, but it was a good kind of hurt. I could tell he was into it though, that he caught the bug. The sunlight dappled the trail that split off and meandered through the three-thousand-acre reserve that ran adjacent to the farm. Mercutio pranced and showed off for the new guy riding Ezekiel, old Zeke giving Merc a disdainful side-eye. *Uh-huh, you're bad . . .*

After the ride, the events of a few weeks ago were packed up, stored away with everything else. Only the moment was real—like every other time I was on Merc's back.

Mark said he'd really like to do this regularly. He could

feel the tension draining out of him. It was no surprise to me. It was simply good juju. "No payment required," I said, smiling, "except for some hay and oats. Oh, and $300 a month for board, then shots, dentistry, hoof trimming, tack, and other extras . . ."

Mark laughed.

"It helps if you have your own spread. I really miss that, but it's the only thing I miss. After all, it belonged to my parents, so it was special to me way beyond just a fancy house and land. It will always be tainted now—cursed."

After we finished walking out, untacking, and grooming the boys, we said our farewells. I gave both guys some oat treats. Mark thanked Becky and Zeke for their hospitality. Becky ran her fingers through her short carroty hair, said it was her pleasure and to come back soon. Mercutio stared out at us over his stall, called out to me as we pulled out.

I was silent for a while, thinking about the ending of a poem Khalika left me after I had just acquired Mercutio. I was so high on him then, a kite in a gale. On his back, I discarded the mask until I dismounted and was plunged back into the maelstrom.

And all I ask is that you shake the can—toss my ashes—the sum of all of this—over the loamy hole where he waits. There, I might entwine my grateful fingers in his scorched mane, astride this molten medium as he—banner tail aflame—transcends and whisks us past the dreary math of expansion, the lonesome births and deaths of stars, until infinity and beyond is breached.

It suddenly hit us—we were pretty hungry.

"If you can hold out, I know a little hole in the wall in the Village that has great falafel. I've got some snacks in my bag."

He said he could if I could. We drove in, got our orders to go, and ate them on a bench, under an oak, the aroma of the barn mixing with the ground chick peas and tahini stuffed in pita bread. It was one of those cool but sunstruck spring days that make you think Manhattan wasn't so bad after all. After we ate, we made arrangements for dinner at Il Cortile at 8:30, and we both went home to clean up and change.

That day was the happiest I could ever remember being, even on those long summer days with Khalika at my side.

At nine, over cocktails, Mark gave me the ruby studs. He said he'd found them a while ago, when he was sorting through her stuff, trying to decide what to keep and what to give away. His wife would have liked me, he said, and he just couldn't see keeping them.

"Hey, I missed your birthday," he said. The way he looked at me, I almost started crying. He assured me that he wasn't trying to move in, that he just wanted me to have them. I looked at them. They were that color you always think of when you close your eyes and think of red—deep, but not too deep, the red of a pigeon's eye. I put them in my ears, and Mark smiled and said, "Perfect, for a perfect day with a magic girl on her magic flying horse."

I excused myself to go to the ladies' room and stared at myself in the mirror, the ruby studs glowing and winking back at me. I had a hard time getting it together before going back to the table. I didn't even realize yet that I was in love.

"They're so beautiful, I'll guard them with my life."

"Please, Violet, don't go that far." And he laughed.

We ate, then ordered two slices of zuppa Inglese and brandy. I didn't trust myself to ask Mark up when we got home. I wasn't sure if Khalika would be there waiting for me—to admonish me for getting too close to any man, *especially a cop*. All those years on the run had definitely left their mark. This time, it was me I didn't trust though. Something was taking hold somewhere outside myself, yet deep in some unexplored place within. It was catching fire despite whatever I was doing to douse it. And all I wanted was more of whatever it was. I didn't care where it might lead—only that there would be more of it, that I could gorge on it and never get full. That it would burn hot enough to engulf all our pain, all the past, to a cinder—a cinder that would blow away in the breeze.

After dessert and brandy, Mark leaned in, took my hand, and kissed it, so softly, like a butterfly's wings. Then he pulled me to him and did the same to my mouth. And there it was, the dream made real. There could be no denying it now, the smell, the taste, the buzz of him—so alien yet so familiar, like he'd been hovering in the wings of my life all along.

Mark delivered me to the loft, neither one of us trusting ourselves, not wanting to break the spell of the perfect day.

Khalika never showed, and my exhaustion allowed me to drift into a deep sleep that was mercifully free of dreams. I woke up the next day eager to go out with Mark whenever he asked, especially if it included a trip to the north shore. I had forgotten to remove the studs; when I remembered, I put them in a tray by the kitchen sink and stared at them. I thought of a quote by some woman writer, something about the blood at the heart of the ruby. Then I thought of Mark, and the thought went away. I had the day off. There was nothing that could ever ruin the memory of his mouth on mine. He didn't close his eyes, and neither did I.

CHAPTER 17

D etective Bruno and I have been discussing the case, how it morphed from a simple slaughter of two upper-crust empty vessels to a sinkhole of corruption. I brought up Violet's strange relationship with her twin, something I'd been sitting on. A couple of beats later, Lorena looked up from her paperwork, her jaw dropped.

"What twin, I don't know of any twin. What the hell?" She was really caught off guard.

I remembered Violet telling me how infrequently her sister was around, and made a mental note to check it out. With all the latest happenings in the scummy netherworld where I operate, I came to the unavoidable conclusion that this free-spirited Khalika needed to be located. It wasn't something I looked forward to telling Violet. But I knew it had to happen.

Why didn't she tell Bruno? Something about Violet's excuse was gnawing at me—that she didn't see the point in bringing her sister up.

Then, something weird: one day while I was checking out a lead in the neighborhood around Violet's loft, I thought I'd stop in and say hi, maybe see if she wanted to get lunch if she was up. I was about to park and just as I passed the building entrance, I spotted her exiting the loft and slipping her keys in her pocket.

Except, I realized, it wasn't Violet.

And yet it was—an exact replica, except for the blond cornrows. There was something else, but I couldn't put my finger on it. Something about her attitude, the almost visible electricity around her, some negative charge. It was like she was breathing different air than everyone around her, getting high off it. I remembered Violet telling me Khalika sometimes wore a blond *cornrow wig. She had big sunglasses on, and I couldn't catch her eye. I tooted the horn, but she ignored it and started jogging north, moving at a good clip. By the time I could hang a U and catch up to her, she'd disappeared down a side street, and I gave up the chase.*

When I told Violet about it later, she just said, "Uh-huh, welcome to my world."

The lead I'd been chasing up had to do with my baby—I could never give that up. If you spend enough time at this job—this calling—life seems to take on all the elements of a really black comedy, one where some poor schmuck keeps getting hit with one sack full of shit after another, sliding down in it, doing a clown dance to stay upright.

Except, instead of the audience, the gods on Olympus are laughing. Laughing their asses off.

Fuck them all.

CHAPTER 18

May 1985

I'd just gotten home from the Envy. Some heavy shit had gone down there, and the place was closed for a few days. It was my first night back, and on the way home, I got stuck for a half hour after my train ground to a halt, then went black. Finally, the lights came on, and the train lurched forward—again and again—like some wounded pre-historic ruminant, blowing a fart in its wake. I was grateful it was only May, rather than the airless hell it would be in late summer. When I finally made it up the stairs to the loft, I chucked my rucksack on the floor and collapsed on the couch, thinking I'd take a shower later.

A sharp knock on the door made me jump.

It has to be Khalika, I thought, except I didn't see why she wouldn't just grab the key. Had she remembered she needed to retrieve her rucksack? It would be just like her to forget all about it. She always left a trail of her belongings wherever she went—paint, brushes, empty bottles, joint remnants. Sloppy yet meticulous, particular yet vague—that's my sister.

I checked the peephole. The bulb had burned out in the vestibule, so all I saw was black. I hissed, "Who the fuck is there?"

"It's Mark. Let me in. It's dark out here."

"Oh! You scared me!" I swallowed hard, trying to calm down, slow my heartbeat. But I was relieved, felt the still-novel flutter in my stomach. I undid the locks.

He bobbed up and down, like a boxer, holding a bag that

turned out to be cinnamon rolls. In the other hand, he held a
bottle of good scotch.

"They're diet cinnamon rolls," he joked, his smile lighting
his eyes even more. "And I'm only here on business," he said
ominously, in his best fake-cop voice. I stared at him, then
at the bottle of scotch, then at him again. He winked and
smiled, and my stomach did another back flip.

It turned out that business really was why he was there,
at least partially.

He told me that some guys connected to the porn ring
had met their ends in some really sticky ways—guys who
showed up regularly at their favorite hangout—Naked Envy.

"The one you've gotta know about already, Rudolph Bezruchkov, was found upstairs in the office with a syringe-full of
battery acid jammed in his carotid, his dick—sorry, his wee-
wee flopped out . . . what there was of it." Mark paused.
"I hope I'm not ruining your appetite."

Brushing crumbs from the front of my shirt, I told him
not to worry about it, that I was kind of numb to both porn
and gore. In fact, I didn't bother trying to separate the two.

"Yeah, I know, uh, knew Rudy, a true bottom feeder, but
minus the charisma of a catfish and with a complexion the
color of rotten liverwurst. Come to think of it, he even stank
of it, under that nauseating aftershave. Do you have any idea
who the doer was?"

"Not really. Were you in there at the time? Did you hear
anything?"

I was starving, wolfing down my pastry. I shook my head,
went to get some glasses and ice for the scotch.

"No, I saw the yellow tape, came back here."

Mark asked if my sister had been around, and I told him
not lately, that she might have been around, but not when I
was here. I showed him the painting, with the burnt vegeta-
tion and the hidden Pan-like figure.

"The painting is beautiful . . . and strange."

"Yeah, strange. Anyway, she didn't leave any of her junk around if she did. She hasn't shown up at the Envy either, except I thought I saw her one night. That's who I thought it was when you knocked. She's kind of overdue for a visit."

"Another clunk turned up too, in the same week, and nobody knows if there's more. The girls speculated that the caper at the Envy might have been Rudy's wife, who was known to have a vicious temper and more than one screw loose. She knew he was doing three or four dancers. Plenty of the girls did more than dance. Everybody knew that."

"I didn't know what went down until it came out in the news, after I couldn't get in the place for my shift."

I noticed that Mark's eyes were puffy, blue semicircles beneath the bright green.

"Both low lives were either minor or major players in the kiddie ring. As for Rudy? One hand had been severed, postmortem, and is missing. The other, also severed, was holding his junk. It was all frozen there, you know—rigor. There was a note, typewritten, that said, 'Sticky little fingers in everybody's pie. Look ma, no hands.' That's a rough translation, because, as usual, the note was in Latin. There's an even bigger kicker. His surname, in Russian? It translates as 'handless.' It looks like whoever killed your stepparents also iced these two. A clerk at the station speaks Russian. A real busy guy, or gal, this one—who leaves calling cards."

"Whoa . . ."

"Uh-huh—you can't make this shit up, as they say. We've pretty much ruled out the wife, even if she did assault one of her husband's mistresses and set her hair on fire. Third degree burns."

"Does anybody have any ideas about who dunnit?"

"Dunno yet, we're reviewing the bug."

I decided to light some candles. I've always loved candlelight. The scotch was doing its subtle work.

CHAPTER 19

When I saw the yellow tape around the Envy on the evening in question, I figured there'd been a knifing or a shooting, or the place had been raided. The dump was shut that night, of course, and for a couple of days after. When I found out it was fat Rudy the Russian, I'd almost done a little dance. I hated everything about him, and he was always staring at me in the creepiest way imaginable. And not only at me—at every other girl who danced there—barmaids too. Whenever he'd walk down the bar with that little red-rooster strut, my stomach knotted up. The thinner I got, the more he stared. When I told Khalika about him, back when I started there, she said she knew he was on thin ice. When I asked her how she knew, she wouldn't say anything except the usual.

"I have my sources, little dancer."

When the place re-opened a few days later, all the shiny suits were paranoid about everybody who came in—even the dancers. Their eyes darted around like pinballs, full of simmering malevolence. They were twitchy as hell and would snarl at anybody who asked them a question, even if it was only to check their schedules.

Mark told me about the other clunk.

"He was a thirty-two-year-old American, we think anyway, one Harvey Garbus. And this is a head-scratcher that looks like a sweet coincidence. Harv was found by the maid, who told us that when she let herself in, the place stunk to high heaven. She couldn't figure out where it was coming from because the guy was a neatnik. His spanking new penthouse apartment was always eat-off-the-floor clean. She let herself in and the odor kept getting stronger. When she got to one of his five or six bathrooms, she found the source of the stench. There was Harvey, dead in the sunken marble tub. It turned out he was impaled on a plunger—stuck right up his ass. Another housekeeper passed out and hitting the deck, but not hard enough to need an ambulance."

"Gaaaaaaah, what the fuck . . ." was all I could manage. "How the hell could that even happen?"

"It turned out to be some kind of elaborate pulley system suspended from the ceiling, one that would lower him up and down, according to his, um, comfort zone. We're not sure what happened, whether he was a regular user of the contraption, or whether he was test driving the thing and the cable snapped, or maybe was cut." He gave a snort of derision.

"He was a hefty bag of shit too, and the whole tub was covered in it, and blood—had been for a couple days. Man, these poor housekeepers. Tougher job than just cleaning other slobs' toilets. This is a double header, a twofer if I ever saw one though. So far, we can't determine whether it was just a happy coincidence or whether somebody followed him in there and cut the cable. Truth is, I don't much care. But that's between you and me and, well, maybe every other cop who works this corner of the sewer."

I stared at Mark, partly because of what he was telling me, and partly because, well, I just liked staring at him.

Along with all this, though, something was emerging of its own accord from a dusty file cabinet, jammed somewhere back in my mind's attic. When I tried to grasp it, it skittered away like a roach behind a cabinet when you turn a light on. I tried again with no luck.

"Of course, the sordid details didn't appear in any of the papers. They just said a businessman was found deceased in his bathtub. They called it a probable accident or suicide and didn't elaborate. The strange thing is, there's no background on either stiff—anywhere. No birth certs, fingerprints, SS numbers. zippo. We're speculating that maybe they were both orphaned early on, and that this has been going on for longer than anybody imagined—deeper and dirtier than anybody wants to know. Anyway, it might be that they got Harvey early—maybe a leftover kid from whoever got iced—and he was too valuable to send off with them. They have special guys to do kids, you know—'cleaners.' Only a handful of the worst of the worst will do it—at least that's what we think. But of course, these 'specialists,' they do exist. Everything does—somewhere, sometime."

Mark paused, cleared his throat, took a drink and rattled the ice around in his glass, shifted on the couch. It occurred to me that every move he made was graceful. He didn't have an awkward bone in his body.

"This has probably been part of a pattern too. We think they might have trafficked him until he got too old, then used him to recruit vulnerable kids on the street from troubled homes and such. Harv must have done a good job, because he got bumped up in the organization. Unfortunately, he wound up crazier than an entire litter of shithouse rats. By the way, the apartment was owned by a corporation. So, we've got at least two dead guys and we've hit a dead end, for now."

Mark suddenly remembered something else. "Oh, and there was another note, crumpled and stuffed in his mouth, in Latin, *aquila non capit muscas*—'an eagle does not hunt flies.' Turns out that ditty is on a piece of stained glass at the entrance of some old cemetery in Minnesota. Weird thing to put at a cemetery entrance, huh? Then, in English, by the doer, 'unless one has no choice.' In this case, we're not sure if there was or wasn't. The note thing, though—it has to be the key, at least to this particular dungeon."

My hands started shaking, and I poured myself another scotch.

Whatever was swimming up, was getting closer. But the roach was too wary, would only re-emerge when it was ready.

The Latin thing . . .

CHAPTER 20

Mark stood up and stretched, walked over to the window, and looked out. When he turned to face me, he looked wistful, as if recalling an old love affair, then disturbed, as if remembering the crash of its ending.

"What will this morph into in ten, twenty years, if we don't get a handle on it soon? It's a multi-headed, multi-tentacled monster already, and just looming on the horizon right now."

His green eyes darkened, turned hard and remote—unreadable. Cop eyes. He turned back to the window.

"Maybe these dead guys figure heavily in all this too, in the snuff end. Girls, really young ones, are starting to disappear off the streets—sometimes in broad daylight. They're finding headless female bodies, the grand finale in the worst of the snuff films. They're turning up in ditches, alleys, in trash dumps around Juarez, Tijuana, Matamoros, Nuevo Laredo, the Sonoran Desert. Some cops seem to be in on it too, but nobody knows for sure."

Mark continued to stare out the window, rubbing both temples with his fingers.

"Shit, I don't know how much longer I can swim in this cesspool. Vice cops don't have a long shelf life, and I get why. But, you know, this is personal. I don't know where I'd be if I didn't have this to occupy my mind. I don't know where I'd put my hate."

Mark went silent for a minute, brooding. I was busy trying in vain to remember what was hovering around the edges of my consciousness, playing its maddening game of hide-and-seek.

Another scotch helped calm my racing thoughts, stopped my hands from shaking. But I was getting sloppy, starting to slur my words.

Mark suddenly snapped his fingers. "Oh, yeah, now I remember what I wanted to tell you."

And so, he did.

After a sweep of Harvey's glass-enclosed lair, he said, they found an earring outside on the terrace, one for pierced ears, but the back was missing.

"It was almost hidden by a plant leaf. They nearly missed it, but it glinted in the sun. Probably doesn't mean much—might even belong to the maid. The slob had a Japanese garden going out there, or his landlords did, thick bamboo and such. Anyway, it wouldn't belong to any girlfriend, I don't imagine. I don't think this dude's bag was women, maybe not even girls. There were no unusual prints anywhere either—just Harvey's and the maid's. The earring went in the evidence bag. Not much else was found."

I continued to listen to Mark, but my mind was drifting. I could almost feel Khalika in the room, hovering like a malevolent shadow. I caught a whiff of her rainy day on a tropical beach smell. I felt that twinge again too, bypassing the anesthetic effect of the good scotch. I tried to ignore it, but it only got more insistent. She was definitely close by, I knew—or was thinking about getting that way. Mark's voice began to seem like it was coming from a different room.

"If there was a doer, either the terrace door was left open, or the doer got in some other way and waited for Harvey to step out there before they snuck inside. If the door had been locked, then they did an expert job of somehow getting the slider open without damaging it. The only way to get access would have been to slide down a rope hooked to the roof after it got dark. If that's what happened. Either he dropped himself or was dropped on that joystick. Take your pick. If whoever it was didn't do it, I can only imagine the reaction when they found him in the tub. It must have been like Christmas morning for Spider-Man—or Woman. There were crumbs on the counter, but it was probably from a sandwich Harvey made before he decided he needed a bath. If the doer made the sandwich, well, that's some mighty cold shit right there."

We both laughed. Our humor was right in sync, right from the start.

"The doorman doesn't work there anymore, so we're trying to track him down. The only other explanation is that Harvey knew his killer. We've got guys reviewing what we caught on the bug that was planted at the Envy now. As usual, there's reams of boring shit—thug-speak—to sift through to find any gold. A real snore fest. These assholes sure love to talk about what they've done or would love to do with women. It's like they're trying to convince one another how straight they are."

Mark returned to the mystery of the stud, and something else started working its way from the prop storage area in my head. I was getting woozier by the minute. The ruby stud earrings—the ones he'd given me at Il Cortile that evening, on our first real date? When I'd looked for them that morning in the dish by the sink, there was only one. I felt my stomach drop when I realized that maybe the mate had fallen into the sink drain. Now it hit me, like a truck: Khalika. She'd been here, saw them, and decided to borrow them. She did stuff like that all the time. I'd look for something, then find it somewhere else, somewhere I knew I hadn't put it. I racked my brain. But why would she borrow just one—unless . . . unless . . . she lost one?

I asked Mark if he had any idea what color the earring was, whether it was a real stone or just glass.

"Nope, I haven't even seen it yet. Why? They've got a jeweler testing it."

I was starting to get a really bad feeling—about everything. The twinge in my spine got stronger still, until it almost made me jump. Still, I was twenty years old, and there was this beautiful, decent man in my loft, long muscle rippling under his mocha skin, a damp shirt stuck to it. He didn't make any move though, and I didn't either.

CHAPTER 21

In old noir movies, when two people are about to do the nasty, the scene cuts to waves crashing on the beach, fireworks, hokey shit to hammer the point home, so to speak. Now, the whole thing is splayed out on the screen—trying to compete with hard-core, I guess. I always want to close my eyes. It makes me squirm, the shucking of clothes as soon as the door closes, the trail leading to wherever the action takes place, the female with her bra still on if she has a no-nudity clause in her contract, the over-the-top orgasms. You're sitting there in the dark with strangers, watching people moan and fake fuck—on kitchen counters, on the floor, up against walls, in cars, on beaches.

All I could think of was Dick, rutting and slobbering all over his latest recruit.

One night, about a week later, Mark met me at the loft after I'd finished a shift. He was quiet that night, had nothing to say about his work. I could tell there was something on his mind—something he wasn't ready to share. He was jumpy, even ill at ease. I decided not to press him. I wasn't exactly relaxed myself. I asked him if he wanted a drink, and he immediately took me up on it. He seemed to want to put down whatever he was lugging around. I knew how he felt.

After our second drink, we just kind of drifted toward each other, as if there was no longer any question, like it had to happen, how it was a mystery why it hadn't happened already. Later, I remembered it in chunks, like one of my disjointed dreams. No matter how many times I went over it—and believe me, I enjoyed doing that—I can't really describe it, only that it was both beyond what I could have imagined, yet exactly what I had. Not like in those shit movies, more like a choreographed dance where we weren't even aware of being separate bodies anymore.

There was no clumsiness, no groping or moment when I felt I was watching myself on a screen or through a skylight from a roof—the way I always dreaded it might be—a bad out-of-body experience. I stayed right there. For me, it was like a journey to another country, another planet, where the only conveyance was our own bodies. I undid the buttons of his white shirt, traced his biceps, his pectorals with my tongue—ran it down the fine line of hair that extended from his throat to the top of his low-slung jeans. He stood still, didn't move until he pulled me to him, picked me up, and brought me to the bed.

I don't know what got into me, where it came from, but when it arrived, I wanted it to never go away. We could have both died there, and it would have been fine with me. His skin glowed in the flickering candlelight that cast our shadows against the wall and ceiling.

I did naturally what I'd never done before.

I decided to call it love. What else could it be? I couldn't imagine another's hands or mouth on me—ever again, in all the time that would be.

Before we fell asleep, I noticed, with a shock, that Mark had several bruises on his neck. I traced them with my finger. "Wow," said Mark, before he nodded off. "That was . . . crazy."

I had no memory of making those marks. I was horrified by them. What the hell was I thinking? Was I thinking? What if somebody saw them? Then Mark rolled over, and I saw that his back had been raked, as if by a cat.

Oh shit, what have you done? Did you black out, have a seizure?

Suddenly I was scared.

"Hey, don't worry about it. I'm a big boy, and I can take

whatever you dish out. In fact, why don't you dish me out some more of that?"

And I did—plenty more. I couldn't stop myself. I felt no warning tingle in my spine. What I did feel were his strong, slender hands on it, from the nape of my neck down to my tail bone.

I didn't know it then, but when Mark got up in the morning to make coffee, he found the single earring in that little dish by the sink—a ruby stud. Of course, the cop in him didn't allow him to reveal a thing to me—not then. He just stashed it in his jacket pocket and made coffee. Then he said he needed to get to the precinct, although he didn't want to leave. He promised he'd see me soon. He kissed me then, and held me so close, our bodies seemed to merge. I was high on him.

That morning, after Mark split, I started to get antsy again. I'd forgotten all about the stud, didn't even remember to take it out of the dish and stash it somewhere. Khalika felt closer than ever, and I knew she'd know what had happened—what she'd warned me could never happen.

"What the fuck do you think you're doing," she'd say, "and a *cop* yet? What's up—you dick-whipped now?"

The previous night was starting to seem unreal, and I almost went downstairs to call Mark to confirm it happened.

After making the bed and getting dressed, something beckoned me toward the little room off the kitchen that I used as a storage area. Khalika's sealed boxes. Why had I never opened them? Why the sudden impulse to do it now—one I couldn't seem to ignore?

Because I never told you to, I could hear her exasperated response. But now something was telling me, like the insistent drip of a faucet, and I couldn't tell if it was her or something else. At least my back was quiet, and for that I was thankful. Maybe she had given up, or was trying a new communication method. But why now, after the dream-like night with Mark? Why ask anyway? Just do it. I pulled a knife from a drawer and sliced through the tape on a box marked "Future Screenplays."

I stared at the contents for a moment before I opened a red loose-leaf folder. It was filled with Khalika's writings, from childhood through to the present, organized in date order, with notations in the margins. The earlier writings were penned in a childish scrawl, but still very clear in their depictions. This was a diary of sorts, but a detached one, where the writer's identity remained hidden, were it not for the authors' names on the front of the binder. The cover had "Khalika and Violet DeLoache's Movie Scenes" written on it in neat block letters. After I finished reading a few, I sat back, dizzy, in shock, my head in my hands.

I don't know how long I sat there, my head swimming, my eyes streaming. At first I couldn't process it. It came in waves, until the full picture swam into focus.

They told the whole story, in lurid detail—everything Khalika had done. Even worse, it was written like a movie unfolding, frame by frame, except, after each scene, Khalika had written, "To be continued . . ." The scene set up, the dialog—just like how she had described that day in Dick's office. That was in there too, just as she'd performed it for me in the barn. The girl in the shower, at the end: I realized it must must have been Khalika herself—doing what she does—what she has always done..

What is a poet who kills?

Here it was—all of it, in one folder, no imagination necessary: how she dispatched Dollar Man, leaving her first note in Latin: *Natura non constristatur*—'Nature is not saddened.' I realized, with another savage jolt, what had been lurking at the back of my mind when Mark told me about the killer's calling cards. I read how Dollar Man had been found in his car the morning he tried to lure me into it, sitting up straight, stiff as an ice statue, the coin on the seat, between his legs. Behind his shattered glasses ("I ground them under my foot, put them back on his dead fucking face"), his eyes had been gouged out; a screwdriver was poking from the hollow of his throat. "The blood," she wrote, "staining his thrift-shop white shirt crimson."

Khalika didn't stint. She told how she'd gone back to where he was parked, how Dollar Man believed that I—her spitting image, after all—had returned for the shiny object. He'd rolled down the window, not believing his good fortune. *I snared one!*

"Hi," she'd said, smiling her gap-tooth smile. "I'm Khalika. Can I have that dollar? I need to buy my mommy a present and I already spent my allowance. I'll pay you back!"

He said sure, fished around in his pants pocket, and brought out the coin, held it up, and faced her. Then he grabbed her forearm. That was when she pulled the screwdriver from under her pants waistband and jammed it in his "pencil neck'" to the hilt, the blood spurting from his fingers onto her jacket, her blouse with the cherries printed on it, into her braided rosewood hair, soaking the pervert and the upholstery in his bomb car. When he quit jerking around and choking and his hands dropped to his sides, she reached in, tilted his head back, dug in and scooped out his "blue marble" eyes with a demitasse spoon she'd taken from the kitchen. She had to work at that, she said, was surprised how much stuff holds a person's eyes in their head. "It's nothing like the movies." Then she destroyed his thick, coke-bottle lens glasses, "just for the fuck of it."

"It's a stringy mess," she wrote. "Like calamari in red sauce, and I started to feel a little sick." She added camera shots, angles, everything. She wrote that this movie should be nominated for an Oscar for sure—especially for special effects and maybe cinematography.

She told how she hadn't been seen, that people don't no-

tice much unless it's shoved in their faces, and even then . . .
she said she could have done back flips in her bloody clothes
and nobody would have noticed. If they did, she would have
said she spilled a bottle of ketchup on herself. She wrote how
she sprinted back to the estate, winding up her scene for the
segue, where she ditched the evidence. She washed the predator's blood off in the pond. Then she went back to the house,
stripped down, changed, and burned the clothes behind the
barn. I never heard her, could never have imagined in a million years she'd be capable of that at her age—at *our* ages.

What she described as "his cigarette dick" flopped out of
his fly, "a deflated purple balloon." Khalika may have been
verbally terse, but in her writing, she was verbose, scrupulous
in her detail. She described how she skipped off the curb that
day just as he'd taken his dick out and was jerking off. She'd
taken him completely by surprise It was near dark, so no one
was around. "Glurrrrkk . . . agggghhhhh . . ." she'd written
for his dialog.

Then Khalika's voiceover: "Huh? I don't understand!
Just hurry up an' go to Jesus, OK, shithead? I think he lives
in Kansas. I'd stick around, but I have a 9 p.m. curfew and
Mommy worries like fuck when I'm late. Oh yeah, and I gotta
buy her that present."

I remembered how Khalika told me, after it came out in
the papers, that he got what he deserved, that he'd never get
the chance again to try to snatch her sister or anybody else.
"Yes," she wrote, "a meal for the flies to feast upon, in his shit
car, with his dead dick flopped out." She'd drawn a smiley face
on the windshield with his own blood. That was in the paper.
I remembered her telling me about it, laughing at the meager
details in the paper. Khalika ended the scene with the Mighty
Mouse theme song, in honor of saving the day. She had com-
posed this scene right before our twelfth birthday—not long
before she split from Hell House, pretty much for good, until
. . . that night.

I had suppressed it all these years, and now it hit me hard enough to knock me backward against the wall. *How could a kid manage it—what had those monsters made of my sister? What had they let loose in the world? How many others . . .*

Then I remembered how I felt after the alley caper—how I'd always thought she was up to no good—how it secretly excited me. I couldn't go on, yet I was compelled to—a robot, reading about those two jocks and their girlfriends. How, after they'd made fun of me one day, a day I could hardly recall, Khalika showed up at Demo's house when I told her they'd invited me to participate in one of their home movies.

"The morons," she wrote, "never saw it coming."

I was near passing out, but I couldn't put the red folder down. My hands, acting independently of my will, flipped the pages, unable to stop reading. She'd done sketches of everything too. She described how, after they'd ordered her to make them, she laced their drinks with drugs from Bianca's massive stash. Then, after they passed out, she sliced their throats and painted their faces yellow to look like the "have a nice day" button. She used a magic marker to draw X's over their eyes and drew frownie mouths on them. She arranged them in a tangle, bloody clowns in mid-orgy. The note, in Latin, left at the scene: *Ars longa, vita brevis*—'Art is long, life is short.'

CHAPTER 22

I stared at the phone Mark had talked me into getting. I guess this is what I get for dating a cop—an emphasis on safety, security, reachability. It squatted there, a black, silent mushroom that might pierce the silence at any moment with its shrill, insistent bursts. A phone usually signaled that bad news was going to be shared, or more mindless chatter.

I went and poured a huge drink. I must have known all along, but I'd never once questioned Khalika, confronted her. I understood that I'd never confronted her because, on some level, I enjoyed, vicariously, what she might be up to—conning the con artists, beating them at their own games. Laughing at them. But after that night in the alley, it should have been clear: *Watching her do what she did made me feel more real, more alive than ever before   as alive as I felt in Mark's arms. I started to think of my life as something other than a series of movie scenes broken only by sleep.*

What I read next—what made me go numb, made my stomach turn over—was what Khalika had done to Tiffani. The former mean girl, Tiffani, had a blade sticking out of her sternum. Khalika had crammed dog shit she'd brought in a plastic baggie into her "fat, trouble-making pizza hole." Khalika finished up, talking to the dead kids: "Now you're *really* talking shit, you stupid, greedy little cum bucket. And you two dumb steroid monsters can blow each other under the bleachers, forever. In football hell."

I read on. I read the scene where she burst in on Harvey and released the flywheel on his apparatus, then cut the cable, just to confuse the cops. On and on it went.

I stopped reading. I had to.

I made it to the bathroom before I puked my guts out. I hauled myself up, gripping the toilet seat, and looked in the mirror. I was lead, tinged with green, my eyes bloodshot. I sat there staring at what looked like a stranger until I found my legs and ran to the phone to call Mark.

But in the middle of dialing, I stopped.

I couldn't tell him. Instead, I took the file and its damning revelations and burned it all, page by page, in the kitchen sink.

There was no need to call Mark anyway. The phone rang, and when I picked it up, Mark said that the review of the tape finally turned up gold. It was a female who'd iced the Russian. It was all there, and it wasn't the crazy wife. It was somebody he'd brought up there for sex. But, of course, they didn't get to it before she gave him the hot shot and watched him careen around the room for a few seconds. She even said, "Whoops," and laughed when he crashed into a liquor cabinet on his way to landing "like a giant tuna on a boat deck."

"Nobody heard a thing downstairs. The room was soundproof. All you could hear was a muffled, steady, thumping bass."

Before he hung up, Mark said he would drop by later. He didn't ask—he told.

"Wait for me."

He said nothing of what had happened the night before. He seemed to be in total cop mode, at least on the phone. Before he rang off, he added the clincher: the earring they found at Harvey's playpen was a ruby—just like the ones he'd given me.

The single earring in the dish in the kitchen.

I stumbled to the kitchen, knocking over a plant, sending dirt in all directions. I looked in the dish. The lone ruby earring was gone. Did I put it somewhere and forget where? I was frantic. My legs gave out and I had to squat down on the tile floor and put my head between my knees. Mark's gift was looking more and more like a Trojan horse and explained why he had beat such a hasty retreat that morning. He wasn't lying. It was business. I imagined him ruing the day he became involved with me. Hating himself for it.

A headache was forming behind my eyes like a distant roll of thunder. I needed an ice pack. When I opened the freezer, I saw something odd and foreign, wrapped in newspaper, like a fish. My spine twitched hard enough to make me jerk involuntarily. Something told me not to pick it up, but my body ignored the warning. With trembling hands, I lifted it out carefully, as if it were hot, and dropped it in the sink. When I undid the tape, and opened the paper, a big, hairy, bone-white hand lay there, a gold band on the third finger.

It's a left hand, I thought, stupidly.

When I managed to haul myself upright, my vision tunneled and I had to hold onto the counter to keep from pitching forward on top of it. Whimpering, I began walking in circles in the small kitchen, an animal in a pen. Finally, I reached into the sink with a paper towel, re-wrapped the Russian's hand, and jammed it down in the trash, under coffee grounds and wrappers. Then I changed my mind and retrieved it. Retching, I chopped it in half with my biggest kitchen knife—using strength I didn't know I had, although it still took a long, long time—and shoved it down the disposal. I boiled kettle after kettle of water and poured it down afterward, retching even though there was nothing left to purge, as I waited for the water to heat up. I heaved long after nothing came out but bitter, yellow bile. Why invent a hell when life does the job? Another imponderable.

My brewing headache dissipated in the flood of adrenalin. I was on high alert now, survival mode. My darling sister was setting me up for a fall—a fatal one. Either that, or she was up to something else. Did her plans include Mark? What I really hoped for, somewhere in the tangle of my thoughts, was that Mark would see the mutually beneficial nature of what both he and Khalika—and me, for that matter—had going on, that he would just leave Khalika out of this. After all, he had more than he could consume and digest on his plate as it was. And as he said, it was getting more daunting by the minute.

There was also the thick slice of skin he had in this reeking game—his little family gone as if they had never been. It's always like that, I understood, even if you love—or hate—someone for decades. All you have left is a disintegrating tape reel, full of glitches. You press rewind, trying to reanimate a time that only exists in the coils of the brain of an ever more unreliable narrator. It's that view from the back window of the caboose, disappearing into the distance, and whatever is to be hovers behind your back. Mark was alive in the same pocket of time and space, and we adhered to each other in it, like diners sitting at an outdoor café on a busy street, all dying together in a deafening clatter of glass and metal after a cab driver goes berserk, jumps the curb, and mows them down.

Mark doesn't know yet about the others . . . up in flames . . . ashes to ashes. I felt a shock of momentary relief hanging on to the idea that Mark might not pursue Khalika, might consider her as much a kindred spirit as I was. I thought of the faint bruises on Mark's neck, shuddered at the thought that I remembered doing it only vaguely, as if in a dream—one where there is a perfect, fate-choreographed melding of flesh and spirit, mingled with violence.

It's good. It's what he wanted, what he most craved—a purge of the prodding, laughing demons that permeate this world—dancing on his grave that is already open and only awaits him being lowered into it, adjacent to his wife, where they will spend all of eternity searching for the lost one. There, in that dank place, only the temporary home of soul and spirit breaks down, feeding renewal, as the spirit soars. He was finally drawn to sex so wild and pure that it can no longer be thought of as an act of love. It is a naked exorcism that, for as long as it lasts, purges all mem-

ory, longing, grief, guilt, and shame. It ignites, immolates all of it—past, present, and future—like the Indian wife of another century who threw herself on the funeral pyre of her dead husband because any future was unthinkable. Did she feel the flames as they licked at her sari, or was she in such a self-induced trance, drugged by it, that she was numb to the searing heat as she approached the flaming mound on the banks of the Ganges?

Exhausted and overwhelmed, I fell into bed, dreamed I was riding Mercutio through a deep, dark wood. I was a kid again, maybe ten. I don't know why I knew that, but that's what dreams do. You know things in them, but you don't know why and don't care. Mercutio went from a trot to a canter, shifted seamlessly to a gallop. In a moment, he dropped down, flattened out and elongated, like racehorses do when they're going all out for the finish—a gait no other horse but the thoroughbred has. I felt us lift off the ground, then sail up, up, and over trees that changed color from vivid green to crimson, then back again. I saw naked bodies, in miniature, spread over the forest floor. We just kept going until we broke free of Earth's atmosphere, of gravity. Sparks flew off Mercutio's body, his mane, his tail, and his hooves. Mercutio kept running, and he did that telepathic thing, like horses do with each other all the time, except his voice sounded like my father's:

"We're going home—back where we came from. We never belonged here anyway. They eat you down there."

We were no longer two separate animals. We were welded together for all eternity, and somehow, I knew this. I arched forward over his neck and screamed, "Take me . . . TAKE me!" before I woke up with tears of joy streaming down my face, the pillowcase wet.

Bring it, I thought. *Just get it over with.*

CHAPTER 23

**Lieutenant Mark Vincente
Detective Notes
July 20, 1985**

Rudolph Bezruchkov/Harvey Garbus murders

On July 18, Rudolph Bezruchkov, who was part of the management of the Naked Envy—and the kiddie porn distribution operation—was found dead in the upstairs office at that establishment. He had a syringe of battery acid in his neck and one severed hand on his penis. The other hand had been hacked off and taken away.

As with the Danzinger murders, there was a note in Latin on a card, this one translating as "Sticky little fingers in everybody's pie. Look ma, no hands."

Bezruchkov didn't appear to have any official existence, no fingerprints on file, no SS number, let alone a birth certificate. From his name, he is of Russian descent, but if he was an immigrant he does not appear to have arrived via any legal channels.

We had a bug in the office of the Naked Envy, so we're waiting to see if there is anything useful recorded by that.

On July 20, Harvey Garbus was found dead in his apartment at 975 Park. We believe he is American born, but again, like Bezruchkov, he is a phantom as far as any official record is concerned. He is believed to have been part of the Naked Envy ring, starting as a recruiter and then working his way up.

Garbus was found in his bath impaled on a plunger. He had built an elaborate pulley system, suspended from the ceiling, to lower him up and down on the plunger. The cable from which he hung had either broken or been cut, dropping him on plunger, killing him.

As with Bezruchkov, there was also a Latin note, this time crumpled in the deceased mouth, that translates to "an eagle does not hunt flies," followed by (in English), "unless there is no choice."

If Harvey's contraption didn't break, someone came in and cut the cable. There was an earring found on the terrace. If an intruder made their entrance via the terrace, they must have rappelled down from the roof after dark. If not, they got in some other way, hid, and then struck. There was also a half-eaten sandwich. There are no fingerprints, Harvey's or anyone else's, in the kitchen or on any utensils, so the intruder must have wiped everything down.

On the Latin tags: we didn't pick this up until recently since it doesn't come under vice, but a few months ago a guy was found in an alley at 41st between 6th and 7th. He had been sliced and diced and left a paraplegic. He says the attacker was a woman, who he describes as being like a "demon from hell." He had priors for rape and child molestation, and another note in Latin was found with him: "Iniuriam furca in fluvium fuerit electus."—"he chose the wrong fork in the river."

CHAPTER 24

I changed, splashed water on my face. I sat on the couch, trying to regulate my breathing. There was a knock at the door. The clock on the nightstand said 12:15. Mark. I needed to get him out of there as soon as I could. I had a sense that Khalika was going to visit soon, that more sparks would fly out of the ends of her fingers, would burn the loft, and everything in it, to a cinder. I didn't want Mark getting a load of her—not yet, and I wasn't sure it was safe for him to be around her. I let him in, but suggested we go downstairs to the coffee shop.

Once we were seated, I waited for Mark to talk. I knew what was coming, but I tried not to show it on my face, in my body.

"Violet, this whole case is getting more and more troubling. More . . . weird."

"I didn't think that was possible." My voice seemed to be coming from somebody else—from across the shop. I could barely concentrate.

"Well, there's no bottom to the universe. Isn't that what the Buddhists tell us?"

"Yeah, I guess. I'd prefer not to dive down that far, but maybe it's out of my hands?"

Mark stared hard at me, then his gaze softened, as if a war were going on inside him, one with no clear winner—so far. Mark reached over and took my hand, and I nearly lost it.

"Bottom line, Violet, and this may or may not come as a shock, I'm starting to think your wayward sister is at least somewhat involved in these latest hits, and I'll give you a rundown of why I think so. And don't get me wrong—I'm glad they're dead, but I can't let personal feelings get in the way of my work, not if I want to keep doing it."

I must have gone white, because he paused, looked at me with concern. I managed to recover myself. The waitress brought our coffee, and Mark continued.

"There's the female on the tape. Khalika looks just like you, so she'd have no problem walking around the Envy—no problem getting upstairs, promising sex, jabbing him in the neck."

I closed my eyes.

"It looks like Khalika's been around. Oh, and there's the surgery on the skel in the alley. We managed to extract from the, um, patient that he was sliced and diced on the night you and your sister had your birthday reunion. He only remembered, he said, because it was the day of his appointment at the methadone clinic. He's not dead, just paralyzed, a paraplegic with a scrambled bowl of oatmeal for a brain. He claims it was a woman, but that she was more like a demon from a hell that hadn't been invented yet. There was a note left with that handiwork too."

Mark pulled a slip of paper from his jacket pocket and read it to me. "*Iniuriam furca in fluvium fuerit electus.*"

"What does that mean? All I got was 'river.'"

"Roughly, it means the victim chose the wrong fork—in the river, I mean. If that was your sister, she's got a dark sense of humor. You both do. You must have witnessed it, Violet. Or at least she must have told you about it? It's OK, I understand why you'd try to protect her. I'm on the fence here, but I've gotta get off it. I don't want to do it without taking you with me. Because the truth is, Violet, that you might be left holding the bag."

Mark reached into his pocket, opened his palm, and dropped two vivid red studs on the scuffed white table. "It looks like the doer got in by posing as an exterminator. We tracked down the doorman. He told us that whoever it was had blond cornrows, seemed too hot to be an exterminator, but what did he know? She wore the uniform and even had a badge with a name on it—which he forgot. He said he did remember that the lady had a couple of bright red earrings on. They stood out against her blond hair and olive skin. The doer was likely let in by Harvey. Then he went about his business. But instead of leaving, she opened and closed the door, but didn't leave. She hid somewhere until Harvey decided it was bath time. Then, I figure, she struck. It looks like she made and ate part of a sandwich afterward and wiped the whole thing down, including the refrigerator and utensils. Why she went out on the terrace is anybody's guess. Maybe she decided to take some sun or check out the exotic plants? Or maybe she just hid out there."

He paused and looked at the earrings. "Anyway, I'm pretty sure these are the ones I gave you, Violet. One was on the dead guy's terrace, as you know. The other one, I had to borrow from your dish, for comparison. They're rubies—Burmese—nice ones, the gemologist claims. Unheated and untreated. I wish I could tell you something different, but that ship has flown."

Then he gazed at me, sadly it seemed, across the table, and I stared back as I felt my stomach drop under the table, through the floor. My mind did cartwheels, back flips.

I lied again, clumsily.

CHAPTER 25

"Holy shit, Khalika must have borrowed them, but why didn't she tell me she lost one? That night, after we left the club, Khalika took off. I don't know where she was going."

He was sure, I could tell, that I was making it up on the fly—never a good idea with a smart cop.

"I won't speculate about what your sister did or didn't tell you or where she took off to. But if she pulled this all off, including getting into Harvey's apartment, well, then you almost have to admire her dedication to her chosen career. But I can't do that. I'm going to have to hold on to these earrings for a while."

He pocketed the studs again. I knew I would never see them again—all I had of Mark.

"The night of the alley caper? Either Khalika hit the bricks again after she left you, or you were there. Which is it, Violet? We're on the same team, but I gotta know."

"I . . . I wasn't there, and if it was Khalika . . . I don't know—the single earring . . . wait! I saw both in her ears that night, I swear to it. She pulled her hair back and I saw them, or what looked like them. Then one turns up in that twisted freak's apartment?"

Had she done it on purpose? Taken my earring, a gift from Mark, and left it at plunger guy's place?

"I know this is a lot to take in, Violet. I'm keeping this on the down low for a while until I sort out some more loose ends. My main focus is on this sex ring, and I don't want to get bogged down in the righteous deaths of human rat shit. But I have no choice."

Mark's eyes hardened again, like any cop who has hooked his fish, is reeling it in. Even if his mission took him to one of the outer rings of hell, he couldn't abandon it.

"How about we talk later? I've got some more things I need to check out."

Yeah, I bet you do. Fuuuck me . . .

I agreed to meet him later that night. I had no choice. Soon enough, he would come to me anyway, and the screw would turn some more. Then, there was Khalika. I paced around the loft, my breath sour with burnt coffee. I sat down, jumped up, paced some more. I could hardly breathe.

I dialed the Envy and got the bartender, Murph. I told him I was sick and wouldn't be able to make it. I could almost see his bored expression, his overdone eye roll.

"OK, I guess I'll dig up a replacement. Try not to do this too much, the bosses hate it."

I apologized and told him that I'd gotten run down and caught a bug. He grunted, confirmed my next night on the schedule, and hung up abruptly. A new manager had been brought in to replace the dead one. This one, squat and muscled, stalked the bar—up and down—scowling, toad-like, beady black eyes, brick-shithouse build starting to run to fat. Why do these guys always overdo the upper body workouts and forget about the bottom half? Why were such random thoughts muscling to the forefront of my reeling brain? I tried to concentrate again, failed.

I had to get out and walk, figure out what to do next. My head hammered, and my spine twitched on and off like a faulty neon bulb. I could feel Khalika's rage as if she were physically present. I knew she might show up any minute to rip me several new ones about Mark, about my foray into her writing, about burning her diary of scripts. Maybe something worse. Now, in just a few hours, I'd have to deal with Mark again too. Mark of the quicksilver brain, the yellow-green eyes, the hot silk skin stretched over taut, long . . . *oh shit,*

195

stop, you idiot! This was the night I'd have to break it off, say I couldn't handle anything long term. He'd need to question me just like any other witness—or suspect.

I threw on a hooded jacket, walked fast all the way to 75th and 5th along the wall that separated the oasis of Central Park from the frenzy of the avenue, the shadows of glassed sarcophagi. There, I ran out of steam and took the uptown express. The train was almost empty. When I got to Harlem, I descended at one of the most desolate sections of the green heart that beat amidst the raging steel and concrete holding tank of both the anointed and the hopeless. Like ancient Rome, it fermented in its own putrid juice, bubbled on under a cloud of animal exuberance and misery.

It was still daylight, but that didn't matter here. The biblical "Abandon all hope, Ye who enter here" should have been printed on a sign at the entrance. But there wasn't a soul around, not a gangbanger or panhandler to be seen. I was the only survivor of a nuclear disaster where yet another rogue strongman had finally pressed the button, done a Strangelove. I thought of Mercutio, how he probably sensed my panic all the way from Long Island. I thought of riding him through that other leafy oasis, where there was no need to look over my shoulder. He had always been where the heart of solace beat, and now there was none to be found. Solace was dead. I thought of Mark's muscled back, like a swimmer's, against the white sheets in the breaking dawn. Both thoughts had served to keep the beast at bay as it strained against the fraying restraints, dripping saliva. Now it was threatening to chew through them and rip my heart out of my chest.

CHAPTER 26

As I stood frozen at the entrance to the park, I entertained the vague hope that Khalika would pop up at my side and tell me what I was supposed to do now, how to repair the irreparable.

Hunger finally made me quit my hike and since I was exhausted and working on a calorie deficit, I took the train back to the loft. I stopped at a bodega to get something to tide me over until I met Mark.

I hadn't noticed a scrawny looking man dogging me until he started making those repulsive noises, muttering obscenities under his breath. I decided to ignore him. He got a cart and started following me down the refrigerated aisle. What, I wondered, was the point of this solitary display? Was it just a reflex, a disgusting, unconscious habit? I advised him to grab whatever he was in there for and fuck off, but he continued behind me, even closer. He seemed surprised that I'd addressed him, but sensed my fatigue and doubled down. Instead of paying for my shit and getting out of there, I took the bait. I picked up a glass bottle of orange juice, spun, and broke it over the side of his head. He went down with a crash into the dairy case, juice spraying everything. A few customers gathered, staring, milling around us in the aisle, amazed.

"What the fuck are you staring at, assholes—call the cops!"

I looked down at the inert, bleeding imbecile, who seemed to be coming around already.

"And maybe an ambulance."

In my fury, the labels on the cans on the other side of the aisle were vibrating, slurring together; my echoing tirade seemed to emanate from somebody hovering above my head. While the manager called the cops, I went and paid for my chocolate milk and headed for the door, telling the stunned cashier to keep the change. I wasn't going to deal with a police report.

"Yeah, he was making sucky noises, so I cold-cocked him with Tropicana. Just jam him in a dumpster and light it on fire. Nobody will miss the lowlife motherfucker."

The cashier watched me exit, his mouth hanging open. He looked like he was about to say something, then changed his mind. A hefty, hot-pink clad shopper gave a brief review of the performance: "Everybody crazy now, everybody hole ass."

I nodded my head in agreement. "Yeah, cleanup in aisle three, one hole ass down."

I kicked the door open and hit the street, my pulse strangely even.

When I got to the loft a couple minutes later, I couldn't eat. My mouth was a gust of desert wind. I forced down a glass of the chocolate milk, poured a scotch, and lit a cigarette. My hands trembled so badly I had trouble holding anything—not from the recent confrontation, but the one that was coming.

I finally fell into another sudden, twitchy sleep. I dreamt I was on top of Mark, riding him like a succubus. I reversed on him without a dismount, stared at my contorted face in the mirror above the dresser, watched as the tip of a red tongue emerged from between my lips, curled up in a sneer, revealing two tiny, pointy white teeth. I turned again, still riding Mark. But now he had morphed into dead Dick, then the guy I'd just clocked in the deli. I just kept bouncing up and down until I came, screaming, in my dream. I couldn't hold off the tsunami picking up speed in my brain, even as I slept.

I got off whatever was under me—a thing that had somehow started spurting blood from its eyes. I made a conscious dream decision to play along. Now it was Dollar Man, grin-

ning up at me, his glasses shattered, his mouth open, displaying brown, broken teeth. Day became night. I leapt off, ran
to the bathroom, looked in the mirror. In the glow of a full
moon, the blood on my face and chest appeared black. When
I ran from the bathroom, I was back in the Westchester house,
in the kitchen. There, on the counter, like a roast hot from
the oven, was Mark's beautiful head on a platter, in a pool
of congealing blood. His once yellow-green eyes stared into
some immeasurable distance, milky and sightless. There was
a half-smile on his lips, from which a giant maggot emerged,
fell to the tiles, writhed there. The head spoke.

I love you, in spite of everything . . . I always will . . .

I woke up gagging and weeping, animated now only by
something unnameable.

*They're all human dildos—the pieces of rubber some women
liked to jam into themselves to get that feeling of being penetrated, overwhelmed, without the window dressing, the fluids,
the bald lies, the pointless, bullshit charade of relationships—the
fiction of craving what degrades, might even consign you to incu-
bate the genetic code of an idiot, to rotting in the tall weeds, or
jammed in a sewer pipe.*

CHAPTER 27

Lieutenant Mark Vincente
Detective's Notes
August 17, 1985

The transcripts of the recordings from the bug in the office at the Naked Envy are back. The murder is on them. There is a conversation between Bezruchkov and a female, and on the tape Bezruchkov—just before he went down—refers to the woman as 'Kali' or 'Khali.'

The earring found at Garbus's apartment has come back from analysis. It is a Burmese ruby. The doorman at the apartment building recalls a woman wearing bright red earrings and dressed in an exterminator's uniform with a company looking for that apartment. He also remembers her having blond cornrows.

The earrings appear identical to ones I have seen worn by Violet DeLoache, the sister to Khalika DeLoache. I have never met Khalika DeLoache, but I saw her leaving Violet's apartment once, and she had blond cornrows.

I've also heard from Lt. Bruno, and it turns out that cards or notes with Latin tags were found with three other murders in Westchester—a pedophile found dead in his car; a high-school teacher at the school Violet attended; and four kids at the same school. They were all before Lt. Bruno joined the department—the pedo was as far back as 1978, and although she knew about them, she hadn't known the details—the police never made the Latin tags public. She found out about them recently after digging through some files and let me know.

CHAPTER 28

I was spent, beyond that. I almost called Mark to cancel unless he was determined to see me. Anyway, I just wanted to get it over with before I had to deal with my sister. I didn't dare suggest he come to the loft, since I knew she might show at any moment, bore into me like a dentist's drill on an exposed nerve. It was 8 p.m., and I'd agreed to meet Mark at Fanelli's at 10:30. I brushed my teeth, rinsing the acidic taste of vomit from my mouth. I was running off what little fat I had. I showered and threw on a stretchy, ankle-length, black dress. My face looked deathly, dark circled eyes floating in an ashen pallor. I fixed it as best I could before I pulled on flat-heeled boots, grabbed my keys, and jammed them in my jacket pocket. I slid a sheathed blade inside my left boot. It went with me everywhere, even on short trips.

On the way to meet Mark, I imagined life without Khalika. I could not. She and Mercutio were all that kept me together, and I knew that Mark was lost to me. All this I knew somewhere beyond my bones. Even Mark couldn't keep me fastened to this desolate landscape without them. Khalika killed Dick and Bianca. She did it to save me. For whatever else she did, I forgave her.

"We are put here to do the work," she said, and that one day I would know that. It looked like that day was upon me, and I didn't know if I would survive it. I knew only one thing for certain: I couldn't allow Khalika to hurt Mark. I couldn't live, wouldn't want to. She had suffered with me, evolved with me into whatever we had both become. We'd struggled from the start to make sense of a world that mostly made none.

"You can spend your whole fifteen minutes in the light

trying," claimed Khalika. "God's—*His*—handbook made you realize why everything is so hopelessly fucked. It's because everybody has to sacrifice somebody, eat somebody—eat everything that breathes."

And women always seem to be left holding the bag. The bloody fucking bag, with all the tools conceived and implemented by man himself. If you're left holding it anyway, you might as well make use good use of it. "*Be hung for a sheep as a lamb . . .*"

I rounded the corner and spotted Mark's car pulling into a space across the street. I watched him alight with the off-handed grace of a dancer. He noticed me immediately and for a moment we both paused and stared at each other over a distance that suddenly seemed unbreachable. Mark smiled at me, crossed over and waited. When I reached him, my weakness and disorientation were such that I almost fell into his arms. Mark reached under my chin and tilted my head up, so my eyes met his.

"Jesus, baby, you look like you've taken a beating. Tell me who it was and I'll fuck 'em up."

He held both fists up, rose up on his toes, and did a few joke jabs. I couldn't even fake a smile.

"I don't know where to start, Mark, so if you don't mind, I won't. Not yet. Just bring me up to speed."

"OK, but I don't think what I have to tell you is going to make you feel better."

"I don't care—I already know too much, and I don't think there's anything that would shock me now."

Mark looked at me quizzically. "Has something gone down since we last spoke?"

"Yeah, but I haven't really sorted it out in my head yet, not in any way that makes sense."

"OK, baby, take your time. I'd rather be in front of the fireplace with you, but I'll settle for looking at you across a sticky table. You know I'd never do anything to hurt you, don't you?"

Mark tilted my chin up farther and kissed me. Then he held me to him for a full minute before he released me. I felt as brittle as a dried butterfly pinned under glass. Once inside the bar, my eyes had to adjust to the darkness and Mark guided me to a table in the corner, ordered drinks.

"Seriously, Violet, and I think you should order something to eat—even if it's a grilled cheese."

I told him I'd already eaten but neglected to say that I'd thrown it all up.

"OK, I'll get right to it."

I heard the words, but I had trouble focusing on what they meant.

"You're too smart to have this fed to you in small bites. What's important is locating your sister, but it looks like we might have a problem with that."

"Besides the fact that she has no known address and is as slippery as snot on a doorknob?"

My voice was so low I could hardly hear myself over the jukebox. It was Otis Redding's "I've Been Loving You Too Long." I suddenly had the ridiculous urge to get up and slow dance with Mark, re-enact a scene from some old noir movie where the bad girl performs her hoodoo on the poor, deluded hero, pulls him into her web of lies and deceit before she dances him to death. But this time, I wanted to change the script—have them finish their dance and walk off together, hand in hand, into the chill, misty evening, me staring up at him in wonder.

"You're telling me you have no way to get in touch with her?"

I stared at the bottles over the bar, then into Mark's eyes. They were deep forest green in the dim light. Even before he went in for the kill, I felt my heart break. Whatever he knew, I knew there would be more to come, and soon.

"No, I never could. It's always been that way."

CHAPTER 29

Everything I'd just seen in those boxes was scurrying round and round in my head like a hamster on a wheel. I knew, but still tried to deny, what Khalika was capable of. She was an assassin who existed without boundaries, without a center—a runaway who'd been off the grid for a decade now, and she covered her tracks with the best of them. Mark rubbed the side of his face, up and down, with his knuckles. His eyes looked infinitely sad, and angry too, another showdown going on inside him. He shifted in his seat, swizzled his drink.

"OK, Violet, here's the thing. You already know about the earrings. I can't prove it. I don't want to believe it, but they're exactly like the ones I gave you. We also know Khalika borrowed those earrings and lost one. I don't need to tell you again where each was found."

I didn't even bother with pointing out that one might have been lost in the drain. It sounded way too desperate.

"OK, what else?"

"We reviewed the bug, enhanced the sound. When the female doer first came in, the knucklehead invited her to sit down and make herself comfortable. He needed to tell her that the couch was made of calf skin. He must have known her poison of choice because he didn't ask her what that was just said he'd pour her a stiff one. Then he said, 'Here you go, Khali—the best for the best.' I think that was when she jabbed him, and he dropped the glass and the bottle, which was top-shelf vodka."

I stared down at my scotch.

"Even if your sister favored vodka, that doesn't tell us

much—especially since she didn't intend to drink it. She didn't even touch the glass."

I told Mark that I only ever saw Khalika drink beer, and that when she showed up at the bar, I couldn't tell what she was drinking, except that it looked red in the light. You could see that this puzzled Mark, and he rubbed his face again, took a sip of his drink.

You sound like a flaming asshole. Don't, just don't. An idiot can see it . . .

"Violet—he called her Khali."

I felt the blood rush to my head, almost slipped sideways off the chair. Good liars need a lot of practice.

"How can that be possible? She never worked there, only showed up occasionally. I dance under her name, but the bosses always call me Violet, except in front of the customers. Are you sure he didn't call her Kelly?"

Oh God, make me stop . . .

Mark continued to focus his dark forest stare on me. "Since you're identical, it's no stretch to figure out how she got upstairs. This party went down some time after midnight, and she just went downstairs and strolled out the back of the place—even left the door swinging open."

My mind scrambled for anything halfway plausible. "Yeah, well, then, it must have been Khalika on the bug. Anyway, if she really managed this, she never told me anything. I don't understand . . ."

I sounded so lame, and my voice trailed off. The bar didn't do checks. The dancers were paid in cash, every night— right out of the register. The Envy was nothing but a money laundry. I doubted if they even remembered my real name— the one I gave them when I got hired. They never called me anything but Khalika.

"Immediately after the jab, we get some thumps and breaking glass, some garbled exchange before he goes down. He wasn't feeling that great by then, of course, so he collapses like a building demolition. Still, nobody got alerted. Too much noise in the front. We have Khalika telling him she was sorry she had to leave the party so soon, but she had a hot date, something else that wasn't clear. Then silence."

Mark didn't wait for a response. "Look, Violet, we need to locate your sister. These types don't play. She won't even see them coming if they figure out who's been terminating their employees without cause. They'll stop at nothing to find her. They have all the tools available to us, maybe more we haven't heard of yet. The ones who issue the orders are way smarter than the ones they sic on their targets. In fact, sometimes they put contracts out on their assassins—just to shut them up. You get this hierarchy, you see, even among assassins. This is the crap that's going on upstairs at the Envy. It's ugly. We found some tapes. I watched as much as I could. I won't tell you what they do with the girls after they're through with them. I also know your stepfather was nowhere near the top of this shit pyramid. Or maybe I should say, he wasn't invited into the depths of the pile. He might have been ruthless enough, but nowhere near smart enough. He never even knew where his orders were coming from. If I'm right, Khalika likely had way more information than he ever did. By the way, how did you two turn out so different? I can't begin to wrap my head around this."

"I don't know. She *saw* more than I did. She always told me about it, though—at least I thought so. Even if she was responsible for all . . . this . . . how would I not know? How could she keep it a secret? You're telling me you think my sister did this—did . . . everything?" I stared down at the table and Mark signaled to the bartender to make my refill a double.

"Let's just say I'm leaning heavily in that direction."

I lifted my eyes from my drink and stared into Mark's, wanting to take the greenness of them with me wherever I went. His voice seemed as if it came from a place that was slowly being bricked over, that I could never again access. I tried to focus on his face. He looked like he felt sorry for me, like this was the last thing he ever wanted to lay on my sagging shoulders. I downed the second drink in two goes and jumped up, tears streaming down my cheeks.

I stumbled, choking, to the exit, knocking over a chair. Mark called after me but didn't follow. I knew what would be waiting for me at the loft. I felt that turn of the screw, more insistent than ever, in my spine. The pain ratcheted up now, coming in waves, until I thought I would pass out in the street. I wanted to keep going—all the way to the East River, deep and dirty with all its history. The pain subsided enough to let me make it to the loft. I looked around before I took the stairs. Mark hadn't followed me, at least that I could tell.

I felt something else too—something so foreign I couldn't name it. Later I realized what it was: my heart was breaking.

CHAPTER 30

Lieutenant Mark Vincente
Detective's Notes
August 18, 1985

Interview with Violet DeLoache

The earring found at the Garbus apartment is confirmed as one of a pair owned by Violet DeLoache. Khalika has access to her apartment and often borrows clothes or jewelry from Violet. Violet noticed the earrings were missing, and that then one reappeared. She assumed that Khalika had borrowed them.

Violet also said that although she danced as Khalika—it sounded more exotic—everyone at the Naked Envy knew her as Violet, so Bezruchkov would never have called her "Khali."

It's now essential that we find Khalika DeLoache, not only to ascertain her involvement, but also because there is no doubt that those at the top of the Naked Envy operation are going to work this out, and she is going to have a price on her head. We have no known address for Khalika, no idea where or even if she works, and even Violet doesn't have a contact number for her.

ACT III

Things every person should have:
- A nemesis.
- An evil twin.
- A secret headquarters.
- An escape hatch.
- A partner in crime.
- A secret identity.

—Wil Wheaton

CHAPTER 1

Come from forever and you will go everywhere.
                                        —Arthur Rimbaud

*A*t this point in time (stupid phrase, as if there is any other *point in which to operate), I believe I've earned my own inner monologue. Sorry to say, there is much to unpack—besides my rucksack—almost enough for another play in itself. But further dithering will get us nowhere. Time to stop posting road signs, or, like Shakespeare or Dylan, nailing time bombs to the hands of the clock. Enough concocting movie scenes to mask the horror, to shield the raw, bleeding psyche from the unmitigated onslaught. K?*

If it's not too distracting, I'd like to request Santana's "Black Magic Woman," or perhaps "Soul Sacrifice" specifically those from their 1970 Tanglewood concert—just softly, in the background. The drums . . .

So . . . greetings, strivers and slackers. I am the elusive, delusive Khalika. I'm sending this out there, on the wind, the same way everyone does, like prayers, supplications when they argue with the will of their chosen god, when they plead with "Him" to no avail. For me, however, there is a twist: it is how I sometimes check in with my sister. Think of electrons, inextricably entangled, whatever the distance separating us. Sometimes my messages don't penetrate the static, the dreary detritus of existence. That's when I have to give her a pinch or, if that fails, show up in person—a cameo, for movie buffs like us. But I'm pretty certain Violet has already filled you in on the particulars of my methodology by now. It has not been easy for the poor child, I admit. I can't monitor everything; even I have to recharge the batteries, check out to regroup. Even vampires have to do that. This twin thing is tricky enough in the best of circumstances. But I—we!—are getting better all the time.

The showing up part: it takes much psychic energy—on both our parts—and challenges my determination not to reveal more than she can assimilate; thus, the infrequency and timing of my visitations. You might consider me the quintessential buzzkill, but no matter. And, anyway, it isn't true. It's a wicked world beyond the confines of your abode, and you need quite a bag of tools to navigate it, hold it at bay, without winding up on a slab—in a ditch, a stream, a dumpster, a plastic picnic cooler, a suitcase—before your time.

Whatever your conclusions about me, your outraged adjudications, know that they do not concern me in the least, do not make a ripple in the clear sea of my destiny. I, as co-narrator, call the shots, and you may believe whatever gives you comfort in a lawless universe. And by "lawless," I don't mean an absence of the blunt physical laws governing expansion, the birth and death of stars, the existence of light as wave and particle, all the numberless mysteries yet to be contemplated and set in cosmological stone. I mean the essential, eternal detachment from anything that happens to us on this hurtling cinder. I don't mean to burst any metaphysical bubbles, but really, it's time to face the music of the spheres without the guiding hand of a Heavenly Father. Humans and roaches are on equal footing here, no matter what people tell you, or themselves, what they whistle in the dark—except in the eyes of human law.

Myself? I am but a vessel of lawless potential, a chunk of the roaring engine that gave rise to whatever I am. I didn't get this far in this round by hiding my light under a bushel. My sister: I am not Violet any more than she is I, although we are inseparable, both temporally and eternally. Even if you believe that my ends don't justify my means, you can at least admit that my and my sister's childhoods have not been optimal, but that under my tender tutelage, we have made the best of it, perhaps more than that.

So, let's leave it at that. I make no apologies for myself, and never will. Life is cheap and getting more so at the dawn of each new day as we lurch toward a daunting new millennium. You might ask, like some dull child: "Are you some sort of demon?" Hardly. That's another utterly lame construct by those who insist on the twin illusions of good and evil, light and shadow, feminine and masculine—of any and all pointless bifurcations, dualities, childish illusions. Never forget that evil, in all its configurations, may only have been conceived in the mind of, may only exist by the grace of—wait for it—your own personal God. With His official stamp of approval. But whatever you may believe about yours truly, I consider myself a bringer of light (think of Lucifer), and a self-styled connoisseur of the gory, 10,000-year-old, murderous carnival. Just think of where that word came from—carnival.

Sorry for the digression. On the bright side, I am getting more efficient at the communication thing, as is my sister—even if she is not entirely aware of it. At the moment, I understand her conviction that she cannot survive any more of this upheaval, my incessant meddling in her free will, her nascent love life. All I can say is that one cannot reveal everything in an indigestible lump, nor can one make an omelet without cracking some eggs. Again, apologies for the cliché, but the egg has great meaning to me, as well as pan-cultural significance. After all, we emerged, together, from the same one. As I said, the bitter medicine, the near fatal knowledge, must be delivered carefully, incrementally, always bearing in mind the fragility, the vulnerability of the disciple—in her case, the dearest twin anyone could ask for. We have both endured much—have made impressive progress down a road where steel-jawed traps are carefully placed in mesmerizing gardens of delight where you either lie there, wounded, waiting for the coup de grace—or get busy chewing your leg off.

Is it not also so, that the fully realized human animal must survive the consuming fires of individuation to become the self-realized Golden Child? It's a tall order. Anyway, that's what Jung thought, and I'm down with it. There are no shortcuts either. Read up if you're interested, but I must warn you: that Red Book is some heavy weather. But isn't everything that brings knowledge, *that leads to wisdom? We are here to uncover what lies beyond the main tent, behind the curtain of the sideshow. We are here to delve, to expose. Of course, it ain't for everyone. It never will be.*

Praxis makes perfect; after all, we've only been together about a quarter of a human lifetime, or more, if you meet up with the wrong stranger, step off the wrong curb, or suck up too much car exhaust or second-hand smoke, ingest too much plastic. But then we have to get into the mind fuck of whether any of us ever had any choice in the matter. I'm not going there, so relax. Violet once asked me what was up with all the mystery, why I can't just give it to her straight up. I didn't quite know how to answer. What's up with any of it? What's jerking the strings? I always regretted the waffling, the cryptic replies, the equivocation. But all of it was necessary—to do what must be done, for as long a time as we are allotted.

I tried to explain that I see everything as if it were all happening at once—present, future, and past—how the reverberations of each affects the other, for better or worse. It's not like I can see into the future—nothing like that—more like sense vibrations from it. But isn't that what reverberations are—vibrations of something that already happened, echoes? The past, to me, explains the way things are, in a constant stream of broken images. Then there's the indivisible instant, the only one anybody is guaranteed. As they tick down, they throw out indicators, signals of what's ahead, like radar. It's crunch time now—for anybody and everything. Take it to the bank. All the end-times lunatics are finally having their way. But they don't seem pleased, I must say—don't seem delirious about going to meet Jesus. In fact, they seem to be shitting themselves.

Anyway, all this speaks to me in a language defiant of translation. I hope to be able to know, someday, exactly how this came to be, but won't hold my breath, so to speak. Early on, after I tried to explain this to Violet—badly, I'm afraid—she asked, "So, we're not even in charge of what we do next? Of what we think next?"

I made an attempt to indulge her.

"Just pretend that I'm God, but that my methodology is a bit more refined, more particular, less slash and burn. Of course, I would never have let it all get this far in the first place. I mean, before pulling the plug. Something is asleep at the wheel or got drunk and drove off the cosmic cliff."

She stared into the middle distance, which is our way, then seemed satisfied.

Now the time has come to pull the gauze curtain back, deliver the news to my sister—to preserve her sanity in an insane world, in the cruel fiction that has been concocted only by those who stand to benefit from it, to explain that there is so much still to do. I am compelled to fulfill my nature (as if there is any alternative)—instant by instant. It's the only way forward. Stasis is death, the waiting for things to be made right by some external force, by some hero riding across some ransacked plain to save the human day—waiting for it all to be made crystalline in the beyond. Right before the sun goes red giant and consumes what Dickinson called "the experiment in green" (which is no longer all that green)—within that fraction, when everything ignites, burns, and is plunged into darkness again, all anybody ever knew about anything—the entire library—will go out with it, the ashes spread elsewhere. In the meantime, in absentia lucis, tenebrarum valet: in the absence of light, darkness prevails.

Heavy, huh? Like mercury. I admit that even I, a remorseless killer, have to comfort myself at times, suck on a virtual pacifier, when the burden becomes too crushing. In those times, I conjure the image of Siddhartha's shimmering, holy river, and the words of Hesse in the mouth of his enlightened creation, his actor: "He saw: this water ran and ran, incessantly it ran, and was nevertheless always there, was always at all times the same and yet new in every moment! This river is everywhere at the same time."

Every seeker should have that embroidered on a pillow or staring at them from a refrigerator magnet: "This river is everywhere at the same time."

Yes, it's time, maybe past time, to deliver the news, for Violet to understand that from which I have shielded her, what I have made of her: a warrior and a poet—a witness and, finally, an actor. Now, I must try to convince her not to allow a man to interfere with her focus. Perhaps it would become clearer to her what she is—what she always was—if she stared into the mirror, or into Hesse's river—one of any number of eternal archetypes. She would see a face, cloven, like the hoof of a deer. One half would be the familiar one, the mask we wear even when we're alone, even in our most private moments. The other half would be the fierce visage of the Goddess Kali, destroyer of men and, in the fullness of time—in her remorseless consumption of it—the whole world. She would see the long red tongue, extended nearly to mid-breast, the fathomless black eyes, intent on destruction, finally uncontrollable, even by Shiva, who once convinced her to pause in her frenzied death dance. She would see the necklace of men's hands—or skulls—the adornments of her insatiable appetite for death and renewal. Between the two faces would run two strands of DNA, its ladders slurring, entwining in an ancient, insoluble mystery, an implacable embrace never to be unraveled. She would see it all, superimposed on the Sacred River winding into Eternity.

Critical mass is approaching, for everything, everybody. The center cannot hold. I must try to save Violet, any way I can. I must help her find grace on her journey, rather than damnation. I will not harm her consort—our consort.

Meanwhile, follow Hesse's advice: Find that spot within yourself where sanctuary lies.

Because you won't find any out there. I said that.

CHAPTER 2

I took the stairs two at a time, stumbled on the first landing, went down with a thud. When I reached the top, I was near passing out again. I stared at the door for a few moments—couldn't bring myself to insert the key in the lock. Finally summoning the will, I swung the door open and there she was, in the shadows, facing the window. She straddled a kitchen chair backward. The hand languidly holding the cigarette had the carnelian beetle ring on the index finger. The smoke curled and drifted toward the ceiling, disappearing in the eventide.

I froze.

The image of Mark across the table—what I said to him that day in the coffee shop about Khalika being the cat in the dark, then the darkness itself. She, the embodiment of the mythical Rhiannon of the Mabinogion—legendary Otherworld woman, Welsh witch, horse goddess, symbol of the lost, the abducted child. A novel we once read . . . Rhiannon's dual personality. Rhiannon, the darker, occulted version of the protagonist. We talked about what an excellent film could be made of it. My sister, I realized, had gifted me my "fabulous beast," even if he was bought with a monster's money, to rid himself of the remaining daughter of a man he had murdered for it. Had Khalika enjoyed that irony? I knew there could never be such sanctuary for Khalika—not in that house. She planted the idea in our infancy.

"You need a pony," she said again and again, "your very own pony."

She kept reminding me, to keep me, I now realize, bound to the earth, to his backbone, to a place of refuge, to fragile life itself. Within the torrent of inner turmoil, my spirit spoke this to my

*scarred psyche. It acknowledged that it was Khalika who led me
to my Mercutio—or him to me—that near-mythical spirit animal who brought with him light—merged it with the darkness,
welded them together, inseparable. Khalika/Rhiannon/Kali/the
mermaid/the solitary wolf/moon/earth/wind/sky goddesses. How
could I not love her? Ever. All this in a flash, in a split second,
like a wave crashing on the rocks beneath a cliff in Mexico where
we played mermaid, our hair fanning out in the azure sea, and
dreamed of escape across some metaphysical border where all the
filth might be washed clean. Where we would know the faces we
had before we were born into this, would finally meet again our
lost mother and father.*

I sensed Khalika reading my thoughts before she spoke,
my own heart, a bird beating its broken wings against my
breastbone. Then her voice reached my ears, calm, almost casual, yet brimming with portent. It was as if she had only
walked in from an adjacent room, sat down, then remembered something she'd forgotten to tell me, as if facing me
would be superfluous. Her low, hypnotic voice contained
something like pleasure, tinged with weariness, regret, maybe resignation. I had expected recrimination, accusation, but
none were forthcoming. I almost heaved a sigh of relief, a
relief that could never last. Here, there is only reprieve.

"It's been some time, Violet. Apologies for my neglect of
your trials."

No segue—she just dove in. She didn't need to inquire
about my health. She just knew.

A mermaid picked a swimming lad, picked him for her own
. . . "But you forgot, Violet, that in your cruel happiness,
even lovers drown. Yeats said so, don't you remember? You've
become that crazed girl, improvising her music, her poetry,
dancing upon the shore.

"You know, one day this love nest in Soho will be replaced, as if it never was. It will be transformed—perhaps into

a shrine to one of the gaudy gods of consumption. Forgive the alliteration. Oh well."

She took a drag on her cigarette, tilted her head, and blew a plume of smoke at the ceiling before the party began in earnest.

"Miss Dickinson, another of our perennial faves, was a bit of a downer, but she sure could call it: from an ample nation, you have chosen one. Obtrude no more, bitches. Think of how many emperors, or their pet lickspittles, might have knelt on your mat—on both of our mats, come to think of it.

"Well, Violet, I'm not sure how to number this Act, capital A, whether we are halfway into this magnum opus, or whether we are further along, close to fade-out and closing credits. I mean, there could be a sequel, even a prequel. I want you to write it with me, Violet. In fact, I need you to."

Khalika was reeling me in—hypnotic as a cobra. Still dead calm, she turned her head slightly to the left, revealing the outline of her exotic profile, her slightly upturned mouth. She took another drag on her cigarette, inhaled deeply, and blew a couple of perfect smoke rings. My trembling hands were ice cold, even in the heat of the dimming August day.

"You must realize we're both going to die from sucking on these coffin nails."

"Yeah, I can almost feel the rogue cells dividing. Where have you been hiding? I'm going through a bit of a crisis at the moment."

"We are going to have to take a trip down the filthy boulevard of memory this evening," Khalika announced, "and, since I don't want you to step in any shit piles, I will be your trusty navigator. I thought by now you might have guessed, but you are well-armored, my girl, and rightly so, I suppose. That last one was a bit of a doozy for you to witness in your parlous state, I must admit. OK, here we go."

Khalika swung around, throwing one leg over the back of the chair in a smooth, balletic arc, and faced me.

"In one of the sealed boxes, you will find two sonograms. Your wounded warrior must never lay eyes or hands on these items, by the way. Once you've absorbed and understand the implications of these records, you will destroy them, or at least store photographs and such in a locker—Penn Station will do. It's good that you followed my advice to remove those boxes, or they might have wound up in another locker—the evidence one. I did meet *le jeune homme*, by the way, and I can see why you might have gotten lost in him. He is quite the genetic specimen and, well . . . talented. I mean, if this were a script, we'd need to change his name to Jack, as in Jack of Hearts."

I stared at Khalika. "What do you mean you *met* him?"

"Don't fret, little sister, he thought I was you. Remember the marks of passion on his neck and back? I might have gotten a bit too enthusiastic, but I just wanted him to quit with the probing and concentrate on making you happy. But, true to cop form, his work ethic overrode my amatory skills. Sorry I had to resort to such deception. I have never been pointlessly cruel, despite evidence to the contrary. Just read the paper for one week out of the year, Violet, and you know that I speak the truth. The emergency surgery you witnessed saved that girl the indignity of being forced to suck the cock of a bathless speed freak before he made off with what little was on her person, or perhaps left her where he dragged her for the rats to feast upon. Instead, they nibbled on his skanky ass. Rest assured, he remains somewhat alive only by my leave, for I didn't wish you to be implicated in our early morning caper. He lucked out." *What are you telling me?*

Khalika took another long drag. I sagged against the door frame.

"Unfortunately, matters have grown more complicated, stickier. In any case, we must now attempt damage control, lest you implode and bring us both down in a clattering heap. I have kept the truth from you for as long as possible—to allow you to live your life as you see fit, with as few exceptions as possible. Now I must emerge from the shadows in a way you will finally understand, even if it means I must make adjustments to my migratory lifestyle. Incidentally, I must formally apologize for my part in arranging for your entrée into your present place of employment; I'm sure you understand now why it was necessary. If not, you will shortly."

I stood rooted to the entrance. My brain could form no coherent response, no pertinent question. She was right. Khalika had always spoken to me as a sister; now she spoke as if to a slightly dull child.

I stammered: "Khalika, I . . . it looked like you were setting me up . . . and . . ."

She cut me off with a non sequitur. "That gap year you took, to travel and read, is allowing you to catch my references. This is a good thing. A pity you missed a formal education, the opportunity to parrot back what is force-fed you, then figure it out yourself anyway. But I intend to tutor you further, rest assured. You need to get more battle hardened—I mean, with your full cooperation. Sorry to be cryptic; again, you'll soon be privy to all I know, which definitely isn't everything."

Khalika flicked a long ash on the floor.

"Don't worry—you won't even need to wipe it up. I'm catching a chill, little sister; can you throw some steel in that hole?"

I stepped in, trembling, closing the door softly. It was stifling in the loft, and I knew that what concerned her was privacy.

"Nice place, that trattoria. I was almost tempted to join you both but didn't want to intrude on the remains of such a glorious day—a day I wish I had the luxury of enjoying in person. But my situation has its rewards, and I don't begrudge you your little flirtation. Or has it morphed into an *amour fou* by now? All sweet, even momentous, alliances must come to an end, and this one will require a rather abrupt attenuation."

Khalika's cigarette had burned down to the filter. When she noticed, she dropped it on the floor and ground it out under her boot heel.

"Again, no damage, I assure you. You'll see."

Even though I had closed the door, I couldn't summon the will to move any farther toward the frightening apparition facing me. Khalika finally responded to my question.

"No, I most certainly did *not* set you up. Why would I ever do such a thing? Stop asking silly questions. Everything will be patently clear very shortly. We don't have bags of time either, as the English say."

Despite her assertion, Khalika still appeared unconcerned, as if whatever might transpire could be handled, and quickly too.

"I know you've been having some very bad dreams, and when I say bad, I mean fucked up, and that these night terrors are beginning to bleed into your waking hours. Come in and sit down, Violet. If Mark shows up out of concern for your welfare, you must not open the door—for reasons besides the obvious ones. As far as your new temporary job, I know you're almost as big a hit as that six-foot former dude with the marble ass and tits like two cantaloupe halves. That black rose tattoo she's sporting lately is perhaps symbolic of the purest evil blooming in the back room of that den of sport fucking, fronting for the cash cow of kiddie trafficking and dismemberment flicks. I don't think your ace detective is making great headway in turning that cow tits up in a ditch anytime soon. Of course, things can change. You know, you cut one arm off, and another emerges from the bloody stump. I really feel for the guy."

"Khalika," I asked weakly, "what do you want me to do? Did you . . . kill those two fuckers? Was Dick involved with them?"

Again, Khalika waved away the question, continued her monologue.

"Speaking of cash, you do need to stash the dirty money somewhere other than the dishwasher, but that's a moot point now. You do know that stuff is alive with feces, don't you? You think those slobs wash their hands after they toilet? The cop—your flotation device after the plane crash of your, *our* lives—I hope he is not a father figure to you, because he's way too young for that role, even if circumstances have made him older than his years. He is definitely a keeper though—or would have been. But you must know by now that none of them, even if they passed inspection, can ever be that. After all, do you ever get a window into what's behind men's smiles, except, perhaps, right before they slice you open and finger paint with your contents? We both got that window in our most recent girls' night out, *n'est ce pas*, and that Romeo didn't even bother with the smile. I trust he's enjoying his cold turkey and adjusting to his immobility."

Khalika turned her attention back to the matter at hand.

"I have done all the heavy lifting for you, Violet, all the righteous kills. I have done all this for you, for us, as I view the sordid world through your eyes."

"What . . . what does that mean—through my eyes?"

She ignored me, again. "If things were different, Mark might have been the perfect collaborator. I mean, based on his personal history, his career goals, his spectacular ass. Even face down, he's a Donatello."

I was still trying to process Khalika's confession. Translating life to the screen, to the stage, was over, I knew. It was down to the nitty-gritty now.

As I stared at Khalika, transfixed, I realized with a start how much weight she'd lost—as much as I had. Under the pendant light, there were the same indigo semicircles under her eyes. Still, how beautiful, how compelling she was. Khalika's eyes shone like yellow embers in the deep-set sockets above the sharp planes of her cheekbones. I thought of Dylan's song about electricity howling in the bones of a woman's face.

She smiled wearily, read my thoughts again.

"I know—I look like shit before sunrise, but taking out the trash will do that to a girl, even with help. And yes, if you haven't guessed, I am responsible for it all, in a way, including one or two I never memorialized. Remember that math teacher who tried to get in your pants in your sophomore year, who pinned you up against the wall after he asked you to stay after class? His name escapes me—Mr. McGooey? Anyway, the note was genius: 'No math can contain the Multiverse'—in Latin, of course."

I nodded, squeezed my eyes shut, remembering. Before I knew what was happening, he'd pulled out his dick and had jerked off on my tartan skirt. I had run to the girls' room, vomited, then scrubbed the goo away with paper towels as best I could. When I told Khalika about it, she just shrugged and replied: "Well, at least he'll have to give you an A now." A week later, they found him, his eyes rolled back in his head and, it was rumored at the time, his pants down and his dick out.

"OK, never mind. Let's just say he didn't exactly have a stroke. Maybe the wife did, though." She paused briefly before continuing. "Anyway, I'm hoping our predicament will be solved soon; losing that earring was unfortunate, as was the heat getting my name off the bug. All this probing and connecting dots means we must vacate posthaste. Surely Mark and aspiring auteur DB are having a huddle as we speak. This isle of corruption reminds me, like so many cities do, of an aging movie star—all glitter and polished facade over a rotting undercarriage. The haves and the have-nots on graphic display, twenty-four and seven. Soon, even the gated enclaves, the armed camps, will fail to hold back the zombie hordes. These things do tend to run in cycles, but I'm afraid the penultimate one is fast approaching. Take off your shoes, Violet. The Japanese are right about that. And the architecture. And the Zen gardens. I'm starting to rethink Mexico, by the way."

The familiar layout of the loft suddenly appeared alien, the way a familiar room might if you'd taken a tab of acid, ingested mescaline, wandered through a wormhole into a parallel universe in some sci-fi movie. I obeyed her, untied and kicked off my shoes. I drifted farther into the loft, under the guidance, it seemed, of some external force. I knew something was coming that would knock the world off its axis again.

CHAPTER 3

Khalika went on. "Do you remember, Violet, when we were baby co-conspirators—how we'd babble to each other about all sorts of things? No matter; I'll refresh your memory. Once, Dick knelt down and told us that if we did not stop talking nonsense, he would send us to the loony bin where they would put us in teeny-weenie strait jackets and apply electro-therapy to our wee skulls. Do you remember how he always focused on you? No? That's OK, I mean, because I do. Perfect recall is my gift, at least what I'm able to take in, what breaks through the background noise.

"It's the same with Dad, and I realize your recent exposure to his method of communication was a bit disconcerting—but that's another matter. This kind of thing takes energy and ingenuity, and a great store of occult knowledge acquired over centuries. Think of him as another configuration of the Spirit of Nature. Only in the past couple of years has he been able to make contact with me—and only in short bursts. You should feel honored, by the way. I have my theories about him, but they're just that. As for Oceane—nothing yet. That painting I left reflected his presence, that he would soon find a way to get through to you—through all the distractions.

"Anyway, back to dead Dick. That was when things changed for us, and we only spoke in private—in our room, mostly, and later, in the barn, on walks, after movies. Speaking of movies, did you ever wonder why we never entered together, why you entered the theatre first and waited for me in the balcony—way in the back? Did it ever occur to you that I never spoke to anybody—ever—and that in the rare instances when I did, the person didn't reply? Think of Dick and

Bianca: they only got upset when they caught us conspiring, and you learned never to do that in their presence. Of course, I reinforced that taboo as well. Finally, like most everything else, it became habit. You allowed me to take over."

I racked my brain, trying to come up with some response that might make sense, failing miserably. I licked my lips, dry as parchment. I was still trying to process the information about our father.

"No matter. Everything will soon be apparent. I will guide you in this transition and all will be well. Let's adjourn to the library for brandy and cigars."

I followed her like a puppy too early separated from its mother.

CHAPTER 4

V iolet followed me like a zombie without appetite. Her mind was pinballing; I could feel it feel its vibrations, its immobilizing panic. Our twinness, with a twist, sees to it—that our fates are entwined even more so than normal twins. It's our shared comfort and tragedy all rolled up in a tight ball of string that defies disentanglement, that seems to have neither beginning nor end.

I pulled out my switchblade and handed it to her.

She stared at it, numbly at first, then incredulously. Her voice was almost a whisper when she asked if it was mine or hers. "It's both of ours," I replied. "You've been holding it since you came in." She seemed to sag, a look of utter incomprehension spreading across her face, a face that would have been the spitting image of my own, except for the subtle differences inherent in all twins—that indefinable something nobody notices until you're around them for a while.

"You know, little sister," I began, carefully now, "both our birth parents harbored some interesting secrets, but that's in another box. Right now, we must address the one at hand. Let's just say our bloodline is . . . unusual, but still doesn't explain everything."

I paused, switched gears. "Anyway, on a more practical and lighter note, you've been happy lately. And damned if I want to be the one to throw a big juicy fly into the salve of your first pas de deux. Why, I'll bet you're both already having visions of making a couple of mocha babies to replace the one his late wife misplaced.

"As for our genetic heritage, I cannot stress enough how thankful I am that we did not get, through Bianca's mitochondrial DNA, a tainted injection of beurre blanc into the etouffee.

Perish the thought. Bianca, unimaginative as she was, wouldn't have recognized a truly blood-thirsty and diabolical bitch if she took a chunk out of her big, lazy, luminous ass. They certainly were the perfect pairing, it must be said. High school sweethearts who made it on the periphery of a burgeoning industry with an almost limitless supply of fresh meat at its disposal. Our murdered father provided the seed money, of course, but Dicky and his fleur du mal—she of the gargantuan ass and negative IQ—blew it, and quick. Bad as his taste was, he had no qualms about indulging it. And as much as they were at each other's throats, each was the keeper of the secrets that ensured the continued coherence of their banal yet satanic union. But is that not true of so many marriages, so many alliances made in hell, and signed in blood?

"Eventually, perhaps, one of our esteemed guardians would have strangled, bludgeoned, or poisoned the other. I mean, after they'd found a way to rid themselves of us, after siphoning off our inheritance. Like most parasites who lack imagination, they never seemed to know when to quit, never knew when the script was veering off into self-parody. In any case, whatever their nefarious plot, I, with you, beat them both to it. The staging was such a nice touch, if I do say so, another chef d'oeuvre, and one I didn't even conceive of. No less than they deserved and, again, poetic to the nines! The Latin silliness, my calling card, is just amusing lagniappe. Incidentally, that girl in the shower at the end of the 'Asshole Out of Hell' script? That was yours truly. It was a little 'inside joke.' I showered at the mansion after doing the deed. After all, it wasn't like anybody was going to drop by."

Violet, at my urging, had sliced open the tape on the box with the switchblade, then flicked the blade closed. I knelt next to her and touched her face; she almost wept. She still couldn't make sense of what I was telling her. No surprise there.

She asked if we could take a break, go for a walk; she knew what might be coming, what could no longer be postponed. She needed me to tell her what to do, to tell me that she would do *anything to make things right. I nixed the walk—said maybe later, after.*

"I know you've torched my scenes, but there must still be a mother lode of incriminating stuff back there, I mean incriminating in the parlance of our current system of justice."

Violet shuddered involuntarily, stared at me. She was afraid to question me; I didn't expect any rebuttals anyway. Sometimes my graphic scenes surprise even me, but they just reflect reality, nothing more, nor less. There's a reason why death and sex are so intimately entwined: in both, you're one with your victim, lost in the act. A kite in the stratosphere. She set the blade down, rummaged in the box until she found them.

"Do you remember seeing these? Maybe you don't, but the image is buried deep, somewhere beyond recollection. Or perhaps you didn't understand what you were looking at in the first place. Things have a way of floating to the surface though, as you know, like the contents of a septic tank, like Dick and Bianca's work. The one you're holding is the first Doppler, early in our mother's pregnancy. It is dated 8/14. Just look at us cute little sprogs, with our future foreheads pressed together, already conspiring. Under that touching scene, you'll find a later one, in another envelope, marked 'follow-up sonogram, 10/18/64, Oceane DeLoache.' That one you might have missed, and I never thought it appropriate to bring it to your attention, lest you do something rash."

With trembling hands, she picked up the image and stared dumbly at it.

"Don't be afraid, Violet. I would never, in all the time that is, do anything to hurt you, to cause you misery or grief. In fact, I've done everything in my power to spare you those useless, debilitating emotions. What we must do, however, is get out of here before your swarthy swain—oh my!—comes back to check on you. Understand, sister, that what I'm about to relate is meant only to bring you, in real time, to what we are facing, existentially: *utter and complete obliteration. The mission will be aborted, and lofty aspirations will have been for naught. You—we—will be*

confined to an institution, and Dick will have made good on his threat, posthumously."

She held the two sonograms up together, comparing them, until she realized what she was looking at. The first clearly showed us both floating together in the amniotic fluid. The second showed only one.

She stared up at me.

"Now look at your birth certificate, Violet, my sister, my fleur de joie."

For the first time since our infancy, I felt my center go soft, slide downward, as if I had been tasked with the terrible errand of reporting the death of somebody's first born. I watched Violet read what was printed on the document from New York Hospital; it was as if she were trying to decipher something written in glyphs, or Aramaic.

Then the print on the birth certificate: March 4, 1965. The name: Violet Jade DeLoache. The official stamp that certified that she, as is everybody born alive, was the property of the state, one in which it would have a lifelong interest—until it had used you up.

"Where is . . . yours?" she pleaded, her voice cracking.

"Mine does not exist, Violet."

I felt my heart break, almost as if I had one.

CHAPTER 5

"But . . . what . . . are you . . ." I managed, my voice trailing off to a whisper. Khalika's manner of speaking veered from contemporary language to something ancient, almost archaic. It was so disconcerting, it made me dizzy. I had never noticed it before now. Had she always spoken this way?

"I don't know what I am. That is the truth, Violet. I am that I am. That assertion might sound a bit god-like, but what else are we in our own minds after all? How we come to believe we are in control of ourselves and everything around us, all that we deem beneath us, what we slaughter for sport or consume without remorse? Think of our late stepparents. Whatever I am is something that might have always existed. But how can I be certain? JeanLuc has been unable to enlighten me beyond bits and pieces. Whatever it is, is beyond my kenning, perhaps I am a mere idea, and a spin of the cosmic roulette wheel chose only one of us to be fleshed out, the other half of the oeuvre, yours truly, doomed to exist vicariously. Yet even that is not exactly true. But I am in the dark as much as you are as to whether my existence will be snuffed out along with yours, or whether I might one day experience the joy and agony of another corporeal existence somewhere else, or even if I will retain any memory of this . . . sojourn. I certainly have no memory of anything beyond us. Meanwhile, I love you dearly. I can't help it. I love as deeply as I hate. And that is a lot. We are a symbiosis of the highest order—one that contains love, rather than mere survival."

How much more . . . before something gives way, the crumbling dam bursts?

Khalika's voice, the information it imparted so matter

of factly, reached me as if from the other end of a tunnel to
some netherworld beyond even the one I had been navigating for twenty years. She kept talking, her voice the echo of
something that had long since passed through that tunnel,
eons ago.

"At that point, I can only assume, it was too late to change
its mind, if 'mind' is the right word, unless it is the universal
over mind, the demiurge—whether I might be a chunk of it,
an extension of it. I don't know if I exist as a singularity, or
even if there is such a thing. Perhaps this ring should be set
more appropriately with an Abraxas stone."

At some point, you expect a person to clear their throat,
sneeze, cough, or blow their nose. I realized, with a start, that
Khalika never, ever did these things. I don't think it occurred
to her to bother with those voluntary or involuntary functions, to cause me to see and hear them. She was good with
props, though—jewelry, wigs, cigarettes, a cocktail. Which of
us saw to the details, or neglected them? Now that I knew, I
saw it all clearly—how I'd only seen what was necessary, and
ignored the gaping plot holes that were now being closed up
by her as easily as pulling a curtain across a shower rod. The
answer is, there aren't any answers. There are only the un-
deniable, cold facts. Everything—water on a hot frying pan,
fizzing off into oblivion, like the ending of one of her poems.
She had done it all. Through me.

Which of us holds the bag?

"You must understand now why it has always been a *quid
pro quo* with us, why each of us needs the other to survive. As
I said, if you were to meet an untimely end, I don't know what
my fate would be. Just know that I don't act only on my own
behalf, but out of a genuine concern for you—my twin, who
might have been the mirror image of myself, after all, even if
that image has become warped by circumstance, and by . . .
whatever I am. I have done my best by you while fulfilling
my own . . . compulsions? I am sorry, in a way, about our

disseverance. I would have perhaps chosen a corporeal existence, even with all the disgusting body functions, the fluids,
the heartbreak, illness, the farewell to youth and the horrors
of aging. But who's to say I won't suffer all of this as well,
through you? I've often wished you'd quit the smoking. It
seems to be harder to kick than heroin. By the way, only you
had the benefit of getting it on with Mark. I know—hard to
hear, but absolutely true. He did not betray you, and neither
did I. I'm just a master of mechanics."

I was shutting down. I ran from the room, one hand
clapped over my mouth, past weeping, past further questions.
I began to plead, silently.

*Please Khalika, I still don't understand. You are here. You
have always been here. Even when you've gone missing, I could
always feel you. You are what allowed me to stay alive in this mo-
rass, in this living nightmare. You and my Mercutio. And now,
Mark.*

"Violet, it is something so mysterious that, were you to
try to tell anybody about it, you would be confined as insane. When those in power have labeled you, you will stay
that way until they label you as something else or pronounce
you 'cured.' That day is usually when the money runs out. In
vulgar parlance, I am what is termed a 'free rider.' There are
other banal designations: a vanishing twin, a parasitic twin. I
despise these terms; it makes one feel like some sort of leech,
another configuration of a Bianca. It is what they call the twin
that has been absorbed into the body of the other—unless it
is excised after birth. But that is usually an ill-advised proce-
dure. It is almost like conjoined twins, except the free rider
exists as a lump of inert tissue somewhere inside the one who
has prevailed in the crap shoot of life, or in this instance . . .
something else."

My pointless and impotent weeping began again, just
when I thought a lifetime's supply had been exhausted, that I
had depleted the earthly storehouse of grief and shock.

"Please don't cry, Violet. It has its benefits. My so-called ride has hardly been free, however. Wouldn't you agree? Even the most esteemed cosmologists spend their days pondering and arguing about whether the universe in which we find ourselves floundering is, perhaps, the ultimate free lunch—an eternity of one that gives not a rat's ass about the offspring it mindlessly spit out. A perfect universe? Ha! And still no concurrence on the so-called 'big questions.' No resolution to the creation riddle, or even what consciousness actually is, why or how it is. I am, I suppose, just another form of it, whatever it turns out to be. I cannot speculate about where I came from, for then we get into the conundrum of turtles all the way down, infinite regression and other such excruciating mental gymnastics. Maybe it's deliberate that I cannot remember my origins."

My reeling brain somehow processed that my sister was still trying to calm me down, to lull me with her explications, her fancy footwork. She needed to keep me in the moment, keep me from spinning out of her orbit, into psychotic deep space. It was her form of enlightened self-interest. Call it love.

"These questions are no longer important to me, because I can never be anything but what I am. It is like asking why there is something rather than nothing, whether it has all been in service to the twin illusions of good and evil, when neither can trump the other. It's the repetitious argument that frightened, overgrown children have with death until, as Emily put it, 'the moss covers their lips.' Humans are incapable of imagining a world without them, so they hang on far past their expiration date."

"So," I managed, "you don't know if you exist because I do, or if you will transfer yourself to somebody, something else, if I am killed, or when I die?"

"How can I know this when there is nobody to tell me besides JeanLuc's spirit? And even his has trouble breaking through all the human static. I've been waiting twenty years for an answer. Anyway, to simplify matters, I am a small lump of conscious tissue that wouldn't even know what it looks like, would have looked like, if you never looked in a mirror. I can't even, like a blind person, feel your features, the warmth of skin, the weather, except for those times when I inhabit you, when you do not so much hallucinate me, as act for me. That night, in the alley, the line got blurred.

"At those times, you—and I—conjure all my physical reactions, the ones I might have had, reflections of my natural impulsiveness. That's the best I can do by way of explanation. I don't know if I would feel agony if they tried to remove me or not. I don't know if you would, or if you would be carried off, kicking and screaming, to an institution. I am that twitch, the little electric current you feel when there is danger about—existential or potential. That is all I am. It is quite taxing for me too, let me tell you. As I said, no free lunch. But what else do I have to do but wait and plan, to act without harming you."

No! It can't be. You died somewhere, without my knowing, and now you are a vengeful ghost, intent only on taking over my life! Oh Khalika, did I kill you?

Khalika read my mind: "No, Violet, of course you didn't kill me. You have loved me all your life, as I have loved you. And now, you love Mark. The Jack of Hearts stole my sister. Believe me, Violet, in spite of everything, I am glad of it."

CHAPTER 6

The trick I'd always admired—the shot of a character, early on, packing a gun, a knife, a hammer—the one I always forgot about—that's fated to blow a hole in somebody, slit an artery, bash in a skull midway or near the end of the film. Now the flickering screen revealed, in real time, the blunt, cold instruments of death—the blade flashing, plunging, slashing. Yet the distance, in my own mind, was still being maintained. I could not stop believing it was somebody else's conceit, somebody's creation—and that "somebody" was my twin. All the scenes we concocted in the barn—everywhere we went, everything we did. The comfort of the darkened theatre is lost to me forever. Now the audience—prurient voyeurs, ravenous, watching us—rapt, flogging popcorn and candy bars into their slack jaws, swilling soda, tonguing each other, probing with their fingers in a dark, crowded theatre.

"Dick and Bianca were death, Violet. I am life, whatever I have done."

I recalled how free I felt, for the first time in my life, the day they carried them both out in body bags.

I drugged and slaughtered them.

I defiled their corpses and posed them, slung over the coffee table.

How could I not have known? Because Khalika shielded me from it—mostly anyway. She had a job to do, and she would not be deterred. I realized that, in this, I was happy to be her vehicle.

I hadn't even noticed that I'd picked up the switchblade again, had flicked it open.

I almost didn't recognize my own hand holding it, trembling, a dry leaf about to fall from its branch. Khalika eyed me, finally suggested that I close and put the thing down.

Again, I obeyed. Khalika held up her palms to me, told me to do the same. Our palms merged.

"Please, Violet—don't end our production this way. There will be other Marks, other chores to focus upon. As for me, I'm just getting started."

It's like the time I tried acid. My hand merged with a tabletop, went through it to the other side. It was like getting a view into a reality denied to everyone who never took a tab. I never forgot it. Except I'm not coming off this trip.

"See? You, alone, would be incapable of what I have done, wouldn't have snuffed anybody, with the possible exception of those two. With me, you have been able to strike before being stricken, like a pit viper, but with the stealth and determination of a mythological goddess, a shapeshifter."

We dropped our hands to our sides, simultaneously.

"I am not evil, Violet, not in any conventional sense. I've learned to live with this *mysterium tremendum*. I cannot do otherwise. You knew enough, were immersed enough in their filth to finally allow you, with my urging, to slay the grifters—they who would have delivered you to your death without remorse. I was only happy to be of service in that dispatchment—in all the others—before and after, if truth be told. You can say I'm a little over-the-top at times, I'll own that. So there you have it. Although I dislike acting in haste, as Dylan said, the hour's getting late."

Only an hour had passed, at least according to the clock. In that time, another world was destroyed and recreated. There was no further argument to be made. No way to deny the reality of what we were, joined together more solidly than any conjoined twins. I laid down on the couch, turned my face into the cushions. No words could encompass my grief, the terrible knowledge that I could never be the sole navigator of my little boat—whether it foundered on the rocks or sailed smoothly to some tropical port.

CHAPTER 7

"Against all odds, Violet, we've prevailed—at least until now. When all is said and done, you'll understand why things must be this way—for as long as we walk the earth—and maybe beyond. You must see now why there can be no other Marks—no other Shivas. We will always have the gift of instant communication—superluminally—like those billions upon billions of quantum particles reunited across time and space. Einstein called it 'spooky action at a distance.' This unfathomable mystery is perhaps entwined, embedded in our very DNA, never to be unraveled. Perhaps only those myriad gods and goddesses might understand it, those whose fantastic exploits exist only as stand-ins for the failure of words."

She stood, clapped her hands twice.

"We have so much to do, Violet. Without each other, we can neither plan nor act. This must always be our shared mission. You are me; I am you, even more so than ordinary twins. Even if I were successfully excised from your spine, it might make no difference. But if it did, what would you be? Do you think you'd be free? Why bring the curtain down when there is so much to accomplish, real justice to deliver?"

"I don't think I can walk."

"You must eat something, Violet, and I must go, before Mark decides to pay a visit. You know what's coming. I don't think he'll have the heart to take you into custody though."

Once again, I obeyed.

This is how most people make their way through their stunted lives, dazzled by the spectacle, sleepwalkers, hypnotically entranced, mouthing jargon—words of comfort and blame. All the while doing untold damage, jerked this way and that by puppet masters whose faces remain obscured until they, too, are finally sucked down and replaced.

I stumbled to the kitchen, set the switchblade on the counter, and opened a cabinet, searched for something I did not want. I watched, disoriented, as Khalika glided toward the window, her black-booted feet not making contact with the floor. There, she paused, smiled at me, waved. Then, like the willful figment she was, merged with the glass pane and reappeared briefly on the other side of it.

"I'll be back soon to help you pack, and to help dispose of any incriminating items. Tell Mark, if he shows up before you leave, that you must go on an extended trip and that you will call him when you get there. Be brave, my sister." Then, an afterthought: "You know, if this were a series, it would have long since jumped the shark. It's the same with life."

And with that, she was gone. She'd succeeded in making me laugh though right to the bitter end.

There was a knock at the door. I ignored it. In all of this, it was the hardest thing I could remember doing. There was not even time to say goodbye, to find Mercutio and Nimrod a new home. We can never know when any of our meetings might be our last. We rarely say what needs saying, do what needs doing. I hoped that, somehow, Mark might see to it.

CHAPTER 8

What do you call a poet who kills? Call her Khalika, but she doesn't accept any call but her own. I am Violet, half of an egg that divided about twenty-one years ago, counting gestation.

I am my sister's keeper, and she is mine. She has told me what must be done, but how can I ever take from myself what I might have killed to keep—even as I understand that I contain Khalika, that, in a sense, I *am* Khalika, as Cathy realized she *was* Heathcliff.

How can I mourn, grieve such a loss when it seems there is more of both than my mind and body can contain, can ever hope to assimilate? I want to speak to my skeletonized mother and father, long devoured by tertiary consumers somewhere beneath the dirt. I want to tell them that their offspring have engaged in that grim work above ground, of ridding the Earth of living human decay. If I were asked if I believe in the existence of pure evil, then I would have to answer honestly: yes, I do, no matter what Khalika says. I have seen it, and my retina has been forever seared by its images, transferred to my nightmares. What would my dead parents say in response to the monstrosity I contain? I believe I will never know. Were one or both instrumental in it—deliberately or accidentally? I can only put words in their silenced mouths. But the words will not come; once again, they fail.

My dominant twin is entwined in that column of bone and nerve that takes its marching orders from the gray mass of coiled snakes that is the human brain, festering and conniving in its fragile skull.

And what of those jocks and their girlfriends, you might

ask? My sister once joked that they were spared both the crippling effects of football *and* porn; and now, I realize: by our intervention. We pulled the plug on production. Khalika, ever the comedian, laughing into the void. I will take the sound of it with me, along with the feel of Mark's skin against mine, his low murmur after our naked dance, its tender violence. I will take Mercutio's joyful greeting, the aroma of his neck as he pulled me into it, the view of a dappled spring trail through his wraparound vision. I will take my father's touch, so dimly remembered, my mother's face, full of hope, smiling from her wedding photo.

Any incriminating evidence has been destroyed, even if it doesn't matter. Mark will find my note, my attempt to explain what I am.

I am on my way to the sea, mother of all that has or ever will walk upon what has been made of the Earth, her unspeakable beauty wedded to tooth and claw. And then beyond that—to that singular Goddess, that representation of the furious engine of destruction and creation that is the Universe in which we pass the days.

Water . . . Ophelia . . . one incapable of her own distress, inured to the element . . . seeking her salvation through drowning. Shakespeare knew . . . women . . . what are they here for, if not to be left holding the bag, for what men have made of our only home . . . all the burnt offerings to whatever gods they have conjured through all the ages . . . Khalika's poem—that implacable male god clawing his way up Kilimanjaro, scattering the corpses of all that is holy in his wake. I am a container of seawater returning home . . . let there be mercy in its depths . . . rapture . . . like the first time I and my lawless twin first beheld each other in the calm saline sea of the womb . . . the first time I lay with Mark, when the act of love, for once, was not synonymous with death.

As Khalika, I might have planted my foot on Mark's chest, unfurled my tongue between my breasts where the necklace of skulls, of hands, rattle in the wind of my unquenchable rage. He might have looked on approvingly, happy to be my consort on our mission to destroy in order to create. I have eaten our little time, as Kali eats it for eternity, sucking in and spitting out—the cosmic clock adjusted back to zero, where the fresh concert is less than Mozart's opening note, the seed of its idea, a mere potentiality for beauty and horror.

Everything is lost. There is only the driver of the coach. I will put away my labor and my leisure too, for his civility.

CHAPTER 9

Cue intro to Jim Morrison's "The End" in the background. It is near dusk. Mark has not returned.

I am making the trip by train. I sit in the jangling car that ferries me to end of the world. I walk from the deserted elevated platform to the street below. I pass a dingy, decrepit playland, bits of trash swirling around in the salty breeze.

I reach the shore, shuck my clothes, remove the elastic band from my hair and wade into the looted sea of August. It is tepid, has a fine skin of oil on its surface. I would have preferred the numbing cold of January's version. It would have been more merciful, quicker.

I don't get to choose.

I'm already halfway to my assignation.

Khalika's apparition does not intervene, is going to allow the mercy of an exit free of recriminations. Perhaps she is through with me, her spirit no longer willing to inhabit such a recalcitrant and distracted vessel. I swim out, beyond the breakers. My spine is quiet. Maybe she has broken free of me.

As I succumb to the rapture of the final stages of drowning, something swims into my fading vision through the opaque brine. First, she appears as the mermaid of my dream, the image she conjured in Mexico. Her image shifts, becomes that of the unrepentant, yet merciful Goddess of that trash strewn defile, the killing floor, the charnel ground, the image in the alley, in the mirror.

She is my twin, I realize, seen across the ephemeral yet impenetrable divide where we leave our animal carcass behind and merge with the eternal. She is splendid and fearsome, draped in Kali's finery, her macabre adornments floating in the current. Her black hair fans out around her, seaweed en-twined in the strands. *Though you have the will of the wild birds, but know your hair . . . bound and wound . . . about the stars and moon and sun . . . lights fading one by one . . .* She propels herself toward me at lightning speed, reaches out with her braceleted arms and grabs me around the torso. She brings me to the surface. Although unconscious, I somehow see it all from that borderland, hear the familiar guidance of her voice, feel her in the column of my back that ladders down to the vestigial stump of a tail. I hear her low, soothing voice.

Oh no, my darling sister, we are not through yet. I have much bigger fish to fry, and we are only getting better with rep-etition.

I am upon the shoreline, unaware of how I got there, gasping, then choking on the sand. I watch my silver tail be-come two naked legs as my sister sits beside me and leans into me, a hen consumed with her newly hatched chick. She radiates the heat of a raging funeral pyre. She enfolds me in her arms until I cease my gasping and shivering.

Get up and get dressed before you're spotted! We need to get you packed and out of your love nest, or perhaps we'll just leave it all behind. I will acquiesce, promise you a parallel life, free of my mission, until I summon you. At that time, we will discuss all particulars. I will sign it in blood if you require it, but it will have to be virtual.

Then she kneels beside me and whispers in my ear, her hot, insistent breath bridging the narrow-to-vanishing bor-der between all that is, has been, and forever would be. She recites, from memory, the long poem by Alistair Crowley she left for me that night at the Westchester house, before a new world erupted from the ashes of the old, as all worlds are des-tined to do:

There is an idol in my house
By whom the sandal always steams.

Alone, I make a black carouse
With her to dominate my dreams.
With skulls and knives she keeps control
(O Mother Kali!) of my soul.

She pauses in her recitation as I heave salt water.
She cradles and rocks me, continues the poem to the very
end:

There is no light, nor any motion.
There is no mass, nor any sound.
Still, in the lampless heart of ocean,
Fasten me down and hold me drowned
Within thy womb, within thy thought,
Where there is naught—where there is naught!

There, on the damp, gray sand, where so many millions
of footprints have been reclaimed by the relentless, patient
tide, I think I begin to pull myself upright, just as the distant
streetlights flicker on. I hear the rumble of the elevated train
ferrying its oblivious passengers to wherever they are destined
to be. I cannot, for the life of me, tell whether I am dreaming.

EPILOGUE

Lieutenant Mark Vincente
August 21, 1985

I tried to call Violet more times than I can count. Finally, I got the superintendent to let me in. All the windows closed and locked, the loft stifling. I read Violet's note. At first, the words make no sense. I read it over and over, until they do And yet it still refuses to register in my reeling brain.

I see it now. Or do I? Maybe the paradox is deliberate— without resolution? Is it even possible to believe such things? Violet wrote that there are truths that can never be penetrated, that we can only dance around the magic circle.

Will death resolve them? Violet has told me she is a vessel, as is Khalika, that all that is—all we are—is already written.

I don't know how to find her. I don't know where to look. I hope Khalika might do that, in the way only she can. If Violet has given up trying to assert her own will, has chosen death over being subject to Khalika's, then maybe Khalika will stop her—if only to save herself. Violet said that each depends upon the other.

As for me? I am resigned to the idea that I'm in love with, immersed in, something that is perhaps not Violet—yet must be.

I only know that I've been scooped out a second time, the contents hauled away down a river that reflects no light. What is left is a gaping pit, its sides collapsing inward to bury me. Like Violet, I know not what I am, whatever I had been before all this.

The last lines of the note: Si ego non video in hac vita, faciam vos in altera. Non sero.

"If we don't meet again in this world, I'll catch you in the next. Don't keep me waiting."

I remembered it as the ending line of "Voodoo Child," a Jimi Hendrix song so chilling, it was always hard for me to listen to. You believed that young, doomed man really could have chopped down a mountain with the edge of his hand, if only his soul could have rested a while longer in its container.

Even now, in this moment, as it all closes in on me, my mind drifts to our last meeting at Fanelli's. Before I sat down across from Violet, I went over to the jukebox, threw some change in, and punched in some old favorites, the one by Otis Redding, "I've Been Loving You Too Long." I should have asked her to dance. She said we never got to dance, that we should have done that, that she could tell I'd be a good dancer. But I didn't ask her—not in that moment, not in this lifetime. Maybe in the next one . . .

I crumple Violet's note in my hand. I walk slowly to the stove and turn on the burner. I hold it over the flame, watch as the edges of the paper begin to singe, then flare up. Then I drop it into the sink before it can consume whatever is left of me.

ACKNOWLEDGMENTS

Thanks to Sal Simeone and Tze Chun, the principals of TKO Productions, for their faith in me after I presented the mishmash of disjointed, scattered narrative that finally solidified into this book.

Thank you, Amy Sumerton, my "Editing Demoness," who plowed through, organized and made coherent, my fledgling effort—AKA "the beast"—tamed her and rendered her ready for her closeup. She did it during a pandemic, with young 'uns underfoot.

Thanks to Alan Porter for poring over the mess stoically to put the timeline and plot holes right, and writing Mark's notes. He accomplished this in spite of still toiling at his "day job" in the attic, chained to his chair.

Thank you, Dr. Robert, my baby brother, and sister-in-law Dr. Deb, for your input—ensuring I didn't completely mess up the "sciency" stuff, and whatever else. So glad I kept you from drowning that day in Rockaway. Mom never would have forgiven me. I will periodically annoy you all the rest of our days.

Lastly, but not leastly, thank you Priscilla Kim, for your stellar (as in "rising star") cover art—complete with "gems," which is absolutely riveting to say the least.

—Janet

ABOUT THE AUTHOR

JANET PORTER was born in Pittsburgh, PA, and immediately began trying to injure herself by roller skating over broken pavement. Subsequently, the family moved to New York City, where her mother, with a voice that shatters glass, hoped to gain entry into the hallowed halls of the Metropolitan Opera, and where the family lived in a series of ramshackle apartments in the borough of Queens.

Janet has scribbled intermittently for many years, has no writing credentials except those of anybody who has survived, then processed, the daily grind and decided to fictionalize it. That is not to say that every incident in this book is entirely fictitious; it is not. It is merely disguised to protect the guilty, of which she is one.

In writing this, and whatever else might emerge from the twists and turns of her psyche, she keeps in mind the words of the dead guy in the movie *Ghost*, doomed to ride the subway for eternity after jumping in front of a train. Somehow, for her, they apply to writing, or perhaps any endeavor in the arts, including comedy: "You take all your emotions! All your pain, all your love, all your passion, all your rage! Just push it all the way down into the pit of your stomach! And then let it explode, like a reactor! Pow!" (*Ghost*. Performance by Vincent Shiavelli. Directed by Jerry Zucker. Paramount Pictures, 1990.)

Also, "write the book you want to read."

She hopes somebody out there enjoys and finds some value in this offering, a distillation of whatever she has ever read or heard that penetrated the fog. She wishes she could have presented her dad with the first copy. Because all she is, is a chunk of him. Thanks for the books, O.S.C., Chief Petty Officer, USN. I hope you're hanging out with the Bard.

Meantime, write on, y'all!

Janet lives in the Siuslaw National Forest, with her accomplice, five horses, four dogs, two cats, and a murder of crows.

ALSO FROM TKO ROGUE

BLOOD LIKE GARNETS

By Leigh Harlen

Illustrated by Maria Nguyen

A modern-day witch can knit the dead back to life for a fearsome price. Follow a lone predator's surprising night on a bloody hunt. Join a carefree karaoke night with friends that ends in blood, tears, and dark revelations.

Beneath the placid surface of family, love, and reason, the line between monster and human blurs, love becomes obsession, and voices long silenced demand to be heard in Leigh Harlen's blood-curdling debut. Dive into the terrors that lurk behind every corner and in every shadow with these flesh-crawling tales. Contains eight spine-tingling horror stories.

BROOD X

By Joshua Dysart

Illustrated by M.K. Perker

With the Red Scare on the rise and a looming fear of nuclear war gripping the nation, seven laborers gather under the smoldering heat of an Indiana summer to begin a curious project: constructing a bomb shelter . . . in the middle of nowhere. But when the emergence of a once-in-a-century cicada swarm ushers in a series of increasingly unlikely accidents on the site, the survivors start eying one another with more than just suspicion.

A nail-biting murder mystery about the horrors that divide us all. It will leave you guessing until the very last page.

ONE EYE OPEN
By Alex Grecian
Illustrated by Andrea Mutti

After her mother's sudden passing, Laura and her daughter Juniper return to her childhood home in the rural outskirts of Denmark. In the scenic village amidst seas of wheat fields, Laura hopes they have finally left tragedy behind them. Juniper begins to notice something strange about the people she encounters. In tracing her lineage back, Juniper makes a horrifying discovery. This town is alive with more than just nature, and the endless fields of wheat demand to be harvested, whether the hands that do so are alive or dead . . .

An occult thriller about coming home and the monsters that await us there.

WHAT TIME FORGETS,
THE BLOOD REMEMBERS
By Leigh Harlen

The evolution of a vampire. For long, blood-soaked millennia, Jack—and the ravenous thing that lived inside him—feasted happily on humans and reveled in their creations . . . until a catastrophe made him rethink how he spent the long years of his immortality. What followed was decades of manipulation, murder, and bribery while he created the picture perfect family, a completely loyal assistant, and perched on the precipice of becoming President of the United States. But all of his carefully laid plans are threatened when an enemy from his past re-emerges offering an uneasy truce . . .